The Fovean Chronicles Intermission

Book One: Daddy's Girl

By Robert W. Brady, Jr.

Respect is the only thing you can give away for free all day, and yet still have plenty left for yourself.

Daddy's Girl
Book One of the Fovean Chronicles Intermission
© 2015 by Robert W. Brady, Jr.

ISBN: 978-0-9861961-0-2

Cover Art By: Adrijus Guscia
Edited By: Lori Ann Bordner Rutherford

First Printing

10   9   8   7   6   5   4   3   2   1

Dedication:

This book is dedicated to the memory of Amanda Hilliard

You left this place too soon, but made it a better world while you were here.

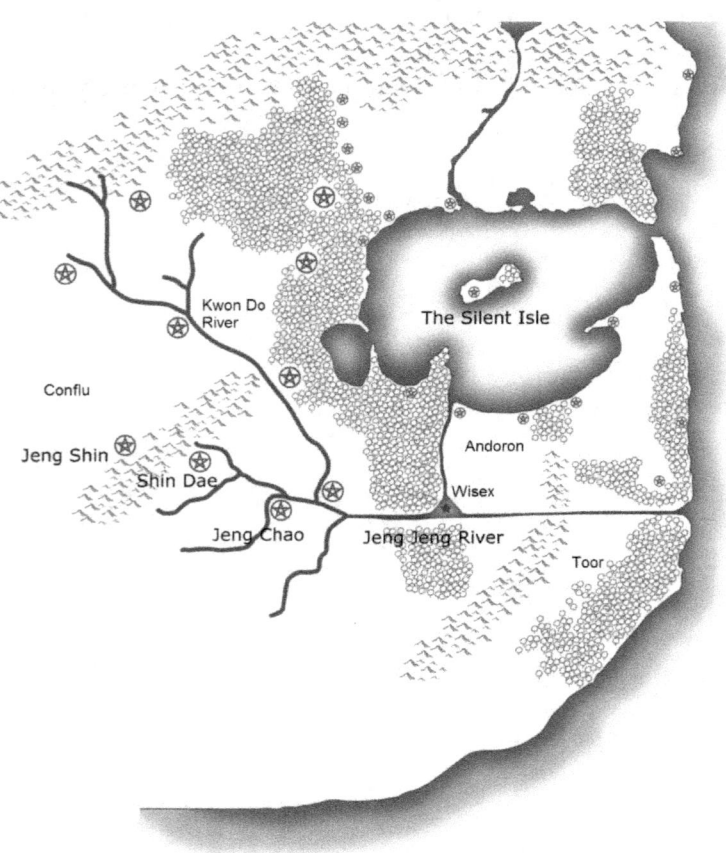

Lee's Map of Conflu

Prologue

Princess Lee Mordetur's heart froze in her fourteen year old chest. She looked into the orb at the center of the room called 'Central Communications,' and she knew before any of them what had found its way into their magix wasn't what she had called 'mama' all her life.

First of all, mama didn't have the strength to step *through* the orb like a portal, from somewhere else to here, and this thing did, along with the power to bring more with it.

Three Uman-Chi leapt out of the orb into Central Communications, a dozen heavily armed Uman warriors with them.

Tartan Stowe, Hectar Gelgelden and her Wolf Soldier guard reacted no slower. She found her person surrounded before she could even think of calling for them.

One of the Uman-Chi, an especially ancient looking one with white hair and an eagle on his breast, smiled like an old grandfather at her. The other two, one with scars on his face, the other shorter and mousier looking, flanked him. Their Uman guards took up a defensive perimeter.

The Eldadorian Uman wizard whom she'd brought with her to operate the portal, ever loyal to Princess Lee, raised a hand white with power, but the old man dismissed her with a flick of his hand. She fell quiet to the floor, not even a whimper from her.

"Angron Aurelias," Hectar spat, recognizing the King of Trenbon. He sidestepped with Tartan to the Wolf Soldier squad as he spoke. "You go too far."

"Too far?" the old man asked him, his voice dripping with malice. "Too far? Your 'Emperor,' her father, sacks my city, sinks my ships, slaughters my allies, and *this* is too far?"

Even mother wouldn't have tried to stand toe-to-toe with the ancient power of the King of Trenbon. Angron Aurelias looked back on nearly 1,000 years' experience. Lee tried to reach into the orb to find her, or the Druid Dilvesh of her father's Daff Kanaar allies, or anyone who might be on right then.

Nothing. The thing didn't even *feel* the same.

Angron turned his attention to her. "I'm sorry, little daughter, but your mother cast her net too wide with this. When I sensed it years ago, I saw how easily I could turn it to this purpose. Every day between then and this has been part of a mission to bring about this very goal."

Lee knew she had to get out of this room. She couldn't fight Angron, much less three Uman-Chi. Her mother had never taught her the more complicated spells for translocation or a seeking, which could bring her to a loved one's side. However, she wasn't without her guile.

Powerful magic had been used to build Central Communications, woven intricately to tune this place to one frequency and to allow others to tap into it. Central Communications existed as a magical conduit between every major city in the Eldadorian Empire, and the capitol called Galnesh Eldador, or 'Eldador the Port.' It moved not only sight but sound, and not only between two places but potentially between all of them. With her *sight* as a sorceress, Lee saw the magix flowing through the marble walls, crawling through a fabric of stone like so many worms.

Picking a spot as far opposite the room's one door as she could see, she extended her will, she reached into the marble, and she unraveled them.

She let the magic run free.

"No!" Angron shouted, and raised a hand to the same spot, taking the power, re-weaving it, containing it from the chaotic expulsion it would seek on its own. Lee's damage would destroy the palace and a good portion of the city if she let it. Uman-Chi lived for centuries – the hybrids of common Uman and the long-dead race of Cheyak. With almost a millennium behind him, Angron Aurelias could reweave what must seem to him to be the simple magix her mother had woven here.

So Lee struck another place, and another.

The other Uman-Chi were wide-eyed. Each centuries old, they knew better than she what it meant simply to release such power from this place.

Lee didn't care. She was a Mordetur, daughter of the Emperor Rancor Mordetur and his witch-wife Shela, a proud daughter of the plains of Andoron.

She would be *dead* before she'd be the hostage of a foreign king.

She felt the sword razor-sharp at her neck. From behind her, D'leer had two fingers beneath her eyes, her left hand over Lee's mouth.

D'leer, an Uman Wolf Soldier who'd been with the family for years. D'leer, who'd washed her hair, who'd been her confidant, who came as close to a friend as a Princess could have.

D'leer, of her personal Wolf Soldier guard. Wolf Soldiers were the sworn defenders of the Mordeturs, Lee's family. While there had been spies in the Pack, no Wolf Soldier had ever turned on the family before.

"Your father will still want you, even if you're blind," the sergeant hissed into her ear. She began to pull Lee from the rest of the Wolf Soldier squad. To her left, they broke apart to pass her.

Except for Hectaro, Duke Hectar's son, whom she'd loved once, whom she'd disgraced since then, sending him to serve in the Wolf Soldier guard. In one fluid motion he plunged his sword into D'leer's hip. The other Wolf Soldiers turned on Hectaro, D'leer screaming, "Kill him!" His father and Tartan Stowe ran to his aid.

Lee pulled her head from the wounded Uman's grip. Hectaro punched D'leer in the face with an armored fist, even as another Wolf Soldier brought his pike down across the young man's back.

Lee saw Hectaro's face twist with pain, heard his father call his name.

Tartan Stowe plunged his sword into one Wolf Soldier's breast, punched another in the throat, then turned on his heel to kick a third. Hectar wrapped his sword up with another, while D'leer and Hectaro both fell to their knees.

The Uman guards charged as the walls wavered under the Uman-Chi's efforts to contain the damage Lee'd done. Lee wondered for a brief moment if that had been too much. Her mother had warned her *never* to affect the magix she and her allies had cast here, even with the best of intentions.

Her Andaron blood steeled her. Lee Mordetur would be *dead* before she'd be the captive of these Uman-Chi scum.

A Wolf Soldier guard engaged an Uman. Another struck Hectar across the back of his neck with hilt of his sword, dropping the older man. Tartan stabbed him through the neck, then abandoned his sword for the pike in the hands of the Soldier who'd struck Hectaro. As the warrior pulled his sword, Tartan heaved the weapon into the back of a distracted Uman-Chi, the mousier one.

The Caster actually exploded. All of them fell back, covered in the red entrails of the dead Wizard. The room shuddered, however Lee could sense Angron had the place almost under his control.

The orb wavered. Perhaps now she could use it to contact her mother!

Hectaro couldn't have been thinking anything of the kind as he leapt to his feet, took her like a doll around the waist, and leapt for it. Almost every being in the room screamed, "No!" as the two of them passed into the brilliance of the altered orb.

The orb had been tuned to the room – the room had been taken out of tune. Lee extended her unskilled will, trying to meld with it, trying to commune with it, trying to discover some way to keep them alive inside of something that wasn't in anyone's control any more.

Still, she thought as her consciousness seeped away from her, better than being the captive of Uman-Chi scum. She couldn't have been prouder of Hectaro if she'd tried.

Chapter One

Potius Mori Quam Foedari

Nothing.

Nothing to see, to touch, to hear, to smell. Nothing like a physical thing, like a deep pile blanket covering her, pressing against her skin through her clothes, smothering her without stopping her from breathing.

Princess Lee Mordetur, daughter of the Emperor Rancor, daughter of the Sorceress Shela, faced with capture by the Uman-Chi wizard-King Angron Aurelias or casting herself into the *space between* reality and the world of magix, would have chosen the latter, had she been able.

She'd been raised a Mordetur. *Death before dishonor.*

Prince Hectaro, son of the Duke Hectar Gelgeldin, her personal Wolf Soldier bodyguard, had made the decision for her. When her private squad of Wolf Soldiers had turned on her under the leadership of the Uman warrior-woman D'leer, he alone had stood between her and capture. When he couldn't win the battle, when he saw he couldn't defeat the Wolf Soldier guard and the Trenboni invaders, he'd picked her up over his shoulder and leapt with her into the void created by the powerful magix cast by her mother and her mother's allies.

She'd called Hectaro *coward* only months before, but when she'd needed him he'd been the bravest of all of her allies, come with her to die.

And Lee had no illusions – she *would* die here. No one unprepared for the raw power of the *space between* could hope to weather it. Powerful wizards and sorceresses could use this to travel great distances, could milk it for power for their magix, could cast things into here which they sought to destroy.

Unprepared fourteen-year-old girls, their breasts barely budding, would have no hope and no chance. The muscles in her back and neck told her she turned her head around to look behind her, but there was no change in the emptiness that her eyes reported to her. She reached for the skin of her face with her fingers and felt nothing, even though the muscles in her arms told her that her fingers stopped moving where her head should be.

She might have welcomed even pain, because then she would know she felt *something*. Lee Mordetur couldn't imagine spending eternity like this.

Though she feared what she might attract, she tried to call out with her voice, but no sound met her ears, even with her vocal chords told her she was screaming.

She couldn't imagine what Hectaro was going through. At least she knew of this place from her training as a sorceress; her mother's apprentice. Hectaro had been taught about horses and swords, not magic.

"And what do I find here?" the thought came into her head.

She started – she'd spoken to her mother through her mind, expelling magical energy as she'd been trained, and so she knew a thought not her own. This wasn't the buttery caress of her mother's mind, every part of it dripping with Shela's love for her. This communication came like warm sunshine beaming on her face. Comforting, but with a sunburn not far behind.

"A sorceress gone astray," Lee informed the voice, another female, younger than her mother but older than she. She guarded her own personality, kept all of her thoughts at the surface of her mind in order to protect the emotions which would betray her.

She felt scared, she was lonely, she felt like she must have been here a long time, and she wanted her mom.

"Far astray, if I find you here, youngling," the voice informed her. She was getting a sense of this one now from the surface of her mind – blonde tumble-down hair, blue eyes like her father's, a woman responsible for many at a young age, who'd recently found both love and calamity in her life.

"Why are you travelling the void?" this woman asked her.

Lee pressed that truth down into the depths of her mind. She'd always known her father had enemies, and those enemies had come at him through her when she'd been an infant in a crib. How much easier to come at him through her now?

She was a Mordetur. She would not allow herself to flee one captor only to land in the lap of another. *Death before dishonor.*

"Your Highness!" the other mind informed her. She would have winced if she could have. Pushing down the thought had brought attention to it. "Lee Mordetur, the daughter of Emperor Rancor Mordetur of Eldador. Your parents think you dead, child!"

She began to withdraw from the source of these thoughts, but couldn't in fact know if she were moving or, if so, if she wasn't moving directly toward it.

"Now, now, little fawn," the voice informed her, feeling closer now. "No need to flee – I am not an enemy to Man."

"My mother taught me how I would be able to identify my enemies quickly if I listened," Lee communicated, "because they would be the first ones to say they were my friends."

She sensed a chuckle. "What a lonely way to live," the other said.

That raised a pang from Lee. It *was* a lonely way to live. Her best friends were her younger brother and her nanny, and the latter was one of the most homicidal people whom she knew.

"Who are you?" Lee asked finally. She didn't expect the truth, but she didn't want to just refer to this other as 'the voice in her head.'

"I am called, 'Vedeen,'" the other said, "I was the Guardian of the One. Now I am the woman of the Guardian."

Lee immediately recognized this truth and, more importantly, she knew Vedeen. There could only be one Guardian of the One at a time, and she'd already met the last one, an ally of her father's.

"You're a Druid?" Lee replied. Her father's friend The Green One was a Druid. Her mother had informed her that The Green One was the most powerful person she knew, other than her father.

The One she knew as the Lone Wood – the forest grove sacred to the Druids, located at the center of Eldador. The penalty to enter that place uninvited was death – if she'd somehow found an overlap between the void and the Lone Wood, she could be in trouble.

"Worry not," the Druid informed her. "Your father is our greatest ally. We would never harm his daughter."

Lee sensed a hidden meaning in that. This woman didn't seem to want to hurt her, but she wasn't the friend to her father that she claimed to be, either.

"Would you have me help you out of the void, child?" Vedeen asked.

Lee knew the answer to that, but she knew the one she *should* give, too. She couldn't know whom this person really was, even though she felt certain that Vedeen was a Druid. Without more knowledge, she might find herself delivered right into her father's enemies' hands.

She would have to decline, and hope to find another way.

"There's no need to suffer here, child," Vedeen informed her, clearly reading her surface thoughts faster than Lee could cover them in her mind. "Your father has ever been a friend to the Druids. We will ward his daughter."

That made logical sense, Lee thought. That alone made it more threatening.

"Am I near the Lone Wood?" she asked. Surely there could be no harm in asking.

Another chuckle. "You are near nothing," Vedeen informed her. "You are *in between*. You are everywhere and nowhere. You are as lost as you are found, farther away from your starting point than you could imagine, and yet so close you could be back there in the blink of an eye."

That gave Lee some hope. If she could be back in the family tower in Eldador, she would be as safe as she could be. However this brought her to another thought.

"Hectaro?" she asked.

Stupid – she realized immediately. Vedeen would know nothing of Hectaro, however admitting that she worried for someone else exposed her to the vulnerability of extortion. She might be able to sacrifice her own life, but of course now this woman would involve Hectaro.

"I thought I sensed another," the Druid said, predictably. "A protector and a seeker. He thinks he might be searching for you, reaching for you in the dark. He has no magic, though – he won't last long in the dark. Not like your other companion."

That struck a note. "Other?" she asked.

Her heart constricted where her breast should be. Had Angron Aurelias or one of his Uman-Chi wizards leapt in after her? Uman-Chi, hundreds of years old, could probably walk the void like she walked the passages of the palace at Galnesh Eldador.

She had to leave here.

"Another," Vedeen affirmed. "I sense her – wild magic, an Uman. The Uman are more at home here, but this one is wounded. Life is bleeding out of her – she won't last long either."

Lee couldn't imagine whom this could be, but she couldn't leave another to suffer, too.

The Druid not sensing Angron Aurelias didn't mean she stood out of reach of his long, thin fingers.

All at once, her courage had fled from her, and she shivered in the dark, a lost and lonely child.

"Yes," she said, finally. "Yes – do it. Help us if you can. Please bring us to the Lone Wood."

She sensed the chuckle again. "I think not the Lone Wood, child," Vedeen said. "I am not there, and it is warded heavily. Even if I inserted you there, my brethren would have your life before they realized who you were."

"Then the palace, please. Where ever you can, out of here."

Vedeen sighed in her mind. "Your father's palace is awash in energies I don't understand. In fact, I was studying it when you flew out, or I would never have known you were here. Druids study the void, Lee Mordetur. We don't master it. Even the Uman-Chi can't control the void."

"Then..." Lee felt her mental voice shaking and tried to buttress herself. "Where can you put me? Can you help me? Can you help Hectaro?"

"I can move you back to another place on Fovea," Vedeen said. "However choices are limited. You were forced into the *space between*, so there is no place ready to receive you. I have to place you where the land and the void are similar."

This meant nothing to Lee. She hadn't studied the *space between*. She knew what she'd done but not what Vedeen was talking about. She also knew better than to confess this to the Druid.

"Here," Vedeen said, finally. "Yes... definitely. I can place the three of you – but not for free, Lee Mordetur. There will be a cost."

"A cost?" Lee echoed. This was what she feared. There were prices a princess of the realm could not pay.

"A cost," Vedeen repeated. "And you shall pay it. A price for you, a price for your guardian, and a price for the wounded girl who follows you."

"I – wait! I don't – I don't know what to do," Lee could barely form a thought. This was coming too fast. "What price – what do you want from me?"

The chuckle again. "It isn't what I want," Vedeen said. "There is a price for you to pay for your birthright. There is a price attached to Lee Mordetur having more left to do than to die here in the void."

"What? No," Lee said. "I – I don't know what you mean."

"It doesn't matter," Vedeen said. "The price is assigned. For you, the loss of youth before its time. For your guardian – he shall not achieve his goals. And for the third one – death, coming after dishonor.

"Yes, Lee Mordetur, I know your family. I know how you feel about these things. I know what it is to lose honor, because I lost it at your father's hands."

This is what Lee feared, she knew. She'd done what she had meant not to do. She'd delivered herself into the hands on an enemy.

"Let it be done then!" Vedeen commanded.

"Potius mori non quam foedari!"

And then the blackness became light.

Chapter Two

A Rude Awakening

From nothing to an intolerably bright light – Lee found herself on her back in a wide, green field, under a blue, blue sky, the sun shining right into her eyes unobscured by a single cloud. She could smell the odor of crushed grass all around her, mixed with the natural perfume of some sort of flower.

She pushed herself up onto her elbows and took a look around her. Hills rolled out in all directions – there could be mountains to the south but they were too far away to be sure. Her people measured distance in *daheeri* - a daheer being one tenth the distance to the horizon. In the hills those distances could be deceptive.

Vedeen's words echoed in her head. She'd said there were three, not two, lost in the void, and one of them wounded. She doubted such a fate had fallen on Hectaro, but until she saw him with her own eyes she couldn't be sure.

A normal child might have called out, but a princess knew the value of quiet in unfamiliar surroundings. Better to listen than to speak – better to have things come to you than to reveal yourself, seeking them.

A normal princess might have stood to see more of the world around her, but a sorceress, even a fledgling like herself, could tell so much more while sitting down.

Lee unfocused her brown eyes and opened her mind up to her power. Her mother had instructed her, "Let the power flow." Find what empowers you, and use it to work your spells.

The desire of others gave her mother her strength. A woman whose beauty broke minstrels' hearts in the nine Fovean nations, if there were men around to lust after her, then Shela could work her magic.

No such luck to the daughter of the Emperor. Lee wasn't a homely child but she lacked her mother's startling beauty. Her features drew as much from her father's severity. His strong jaw, his deep-set eyes and angry brow – these were Lee's legacy. She wouldn't blow the gates off of the walls of Outpost IX like her mother had until she found another source of strength.

Still, sitting alone in a field with no one to worship her, Shela Mordetur would have been helpless as a kitten. Lee Mordetur, on the other hand, could tap into the world around her.

With Lee, it was the growing things. The grass, the leaves on trees, blooming flowers and even baby birds. Lee's goddess, clearly, was Life – the daughter of Earth and Water, come together when the gods fell. Where there was any living thing, Lee had learned to tap its natural energy and weave that into her magix. Now she used natural energy to cast a seeking out into the wind, a spell to circle her in an ever-expanding spiral, until she recalled it or it found whom she was looking for.

She located Hectaro almost immediately. Of the race of Men, grown past nineteen summers and muscled like a swordsman, he still dressed in his Wolf Soldier garb, and he lay sleeping not fifty paces south of her, in a hollow on the far side of a hill.

She found the third person which Vedeen had spoken of right after this discovery; another fifty paces to the north of her, stretched out on her back in the sun and bleeding from her wounds.

Lee rose and turned to the north. Hiking up the front of the skirts of her palace dress, it didn't take long for Lee to find the Uman traitor, the Wolf Soldier D'leer. An Uman with the body of a woman of Men, D'leer had sided with the Uman-Chi King when Angron Aurelias had come to Central Communications in order to kidnap the Eldadorian princess. She'd held a sharp blade to Lee's throat and threatened to kill her, then to blind her in order to control her.

Not every Wolf Soldier could rise to the position of personal guard to the Mordeturs. D'leer had betrayed a lot of good people to do what she'd done, and before her life bled out of her, it occurred to Lee she would want to know why.

She topped one final hill, her blue palace dress with white underskirts and stylish green lace at the hem and cuffs trailing behind her. In the process she stepped on the hem twice – this either needed to be a short trip, or she would want a change of wardrobe.

Stretched out on the ground, her eyes already fluttering, D'leer lay bleeding in her Wolf Soldier greys from a serious wound in her hip. It was anyone's guess whether she was coming out of unconsciousness or entering it. A dark red stain had already spread from her knee to her bust line. Raised in the presence of warriors, Lee knew the seriousness of such a wound – the Uman woman wouldn't be alive much longer.

Lee knew she could save her, but D'leer had betrayed the family and the Wolf Soldier guard. Either was an offence her father would punish with death. Her mother would probably only take longer to kill her.

Vedeen had predicted death coming after dishonor for this one – those words seemed to justify doing nothing.

"Lee…" D'leer gasped, turning her head to the left then to the right. She seemed to want to push herself up onto her elbows but lacked the strength. She must have leapt into the void after them and, wounded as she'd been, Lee couldn't imagine the act of will overcoming the pain required.

"Lee," she said again, and for a moment managed to raise her head. "Your – your Highness. I came… I followed you."

Yes, you traitor, Lee thought. *You certainly did.*

As her father might say, she needed to act fast, or this problem was going to solve itself.

"I betrayed you," she admitted. D'leer wetted her lips as her head fell back. Lee could actually smell her blood now. The sun beat down on Lee's long brown hair.

"It couldn't be – I couldn't," she gasped, and her eyelids fluttered again.

Lee sighed. She'd known this woman almost as long as she'd know Nina, her nanny. D'leer had washed her hair and stood between her and assassins on more than one occasion.

Her father would have let her die – but her father by his own admission had made a lot of mistakes in his past.

Lee unfocused her eyes and felt D'leer's Uman body with her mind. The first thing to do of course had to be to stop the bleeding. She sensed the pain in the other woman, focused on the horrible wound in her hip. She saw the edges of the wound glowing red with pain. She dulled the right nerves, made them blue, then willed the torn edges to reattach themselves. She knit first the flesh and then the skin over it, reconnecting the veins one at a time, inside to out.

Next she drew on the moisture all around her, the late morning dew on blades of grass and flower petals. She drew it in along the ground, building up into a tiny wash, then flowing onto D'leer's skin, letting her absorb it. Water wasn't blood, but she'd need it to replenish D'leer's supply on her own.

D'leer sighed and her body relaxed. For a moment Lee feared the shock of the healing had killed her, but the Uman Wolf Soldier had been cast of tougher stuff. A body slept to heal – D'leer slept now.

She released the spell. It was up to D'leer now. Finally, Lee cast into the Wolf Soldier uniform, seeking out the blood soaked into its dark fibers, and pulled it out onto the ground around her, then out from there into a wide, red circle. The ground would take back the moisture – the spell cancelled itself. What her mother would call 'evidence,' the residual trace of the spell, would be very slight.

"You saved her," she heard from behind her, a familiar, male voice.

She spun, calling up the 'white light' in defense. Sorceresses learned first how to heal, because a sorceress' first responsibility was the life of her tribe. Her mother had taught Lee that her greatness wouldn't be measured in the damage she did, but in the lives she left behind to tell her tale.

But *every* sorceress learned the *white light*, the shining power called from all of the elements as a precursor to a greater spell. When a wizard or a sorceress' hand glowed white with power, it prepared her to call another spell more quickly.

It also scared the wits out of those who couldn't cast – and Hectaro leapt back a foot from her in fear, proving this aspect still worked.

She dropped the spell. Hectaro visibly relaxed.

"You saved her," he repeated, taking a step toward her.

She nodded. Hectaro looked a bit worn, but was still Hectaro. He wore his Wolf Soldier greys, the tunic down almost to his knees with the Wolf's Head insignia on the breast, a thick grey blouse underneath with long sleeves. Grey pants tucked into black boots and a sword over his shoulder, a black utility belt at his middle with a dagger on either side and a black leather pouch next to the brass buckle.

On his right shoulder, a black hook-symbol with a dot over it – her father's mark of the Daff Kanaar.

Hectaro had become a Wolf Soldier to protect her, when she'd hated him, when she'd thought him a coward and the pampered son of a pretentious Duke. Hectaro had joined the Wolf Soldiers, her father's personal army since before he'd become an Eldadorian noble, and redeemed himself. Lee would be dead or worse if not for him.

"She was trying to talk to me," she said. "I – I don't know, Hectaro. I've known D'leer for a long time – as long as I've known almost anyone. She *couldn't* be a traitor."

"Trying to kidnap you might make me think otherwise," Hectaro said. He walked past her, through the circle of blood around D'leer, and squatted down at her left side. He reached out and pressed his fingers into the tear in her uniform, onto the skin over the wound Lee had healed.

A wound Hectaro had made.

"Is it hard to do that?" he asked.

"What?"

"To heal her?" he answered. "I've never seen you heal before."

She did feel a little tired and giddy. She'd been using a lot of magic in the past few months, running the Empire in her parents' stead while her father waged war in Volkhydro and her mother went with him. She'd been doing truth sayings one after the other all day, as well as operating Central Communications, the magic orb every major city in Eldador used to talk one to the other.

Which had exposed them to the wizard King of Trenbon.

"It's not bad," she said. "I've never done a healing that good – um, so intense before."

Hectaro turned, still squatting, and smiled up at her with fine, white teeth, his brown eyes twinkling. Before she'd hated him, she'd had *such* a crush on this handsome prince. Her love had likely made the hatred worse.

His handsome face still took her breath away some times.

"This good?" he repeated.

She sighed and looked away. Making fun of her – he always had. She hated that. He had a sense of humor but this was a time to be serious. She was a princess, after all.

The hills rolled out for daheeri. She didn't recognize this land. She'd been to different parts of Eldador and her mother's homeland of Andaron. This just didn't *seem* right.

"Yes," she said. "Yes, this good. It was a good spell to cast. It's good to know I can I can heal you if I have to.

"You're the one with the sword, Hectaro. You should be glad I can heal you if you have to fight, because I have no idea where we are."

Chapter Three

The Worst Possible Place to Be

The hollow where Hectaro had found himself, carved as if by a giant finger from the side of a hill, became their temporary home. He carried D'leer there and Lee watched over her while he jogged out across the hills to find out where they were.

Her father once told her the world looked flat but in fact was round because Fovea was just a tiny part of it. This thought filled her mind now. She could be more daheeri from her home than she could travel in a lifetime. She might never see her family again.

Sitting there in the grass outside of the hollow, holding D'leer's short, stabbing sword in her lap, she fretted over her situation and over the fate of her toddler sister, Chawnee. She'd been Lee's charge, and Lee had left her in the capitol all alone. Alone, of course, except for 3,000 Wolf Soldier guards, five wizards, Duke Hectar and Duke Stowe if they were still alive, and countless other servants.

She didn't think any of them could stand up to the raw power of Angron Aurelias. If he couldn't take one daughter, it made sense to her he'd try for another, and the nursery just wasn't as well guarded as it needed to be to resist the King's ancient power.

Her sacrifice might not just be for nothing, it might have made her parents more desperate if they'd lost one daughter and thought they were about to lose another.

D'leer stirred a little. She'd been restless for hours. Hectaro had been gone too long and the sun had moved across the sky. She felt hungry and she had no food and no way to get any.

She and her brother, whom her mother called 'Agtani Chewla' or 'Clever Fox' in her native Andaron, used to raid the larder in the big kitchen during the day sometimes when they were hungry and Nina told them they'd had enough to eat. Nina, of a people called the Aschire, was always stick-thin, and the Mordeturs were, if nothing else, heavy-boned and always hungry. She learned to use her magic to pull candied plums and other treats out of the larder. She'd make her brother sing for her and the two of them would hole up in some forgotten part of the palace and share them. He'd make a big fuss but Lee knew her brother loved to sing, and his voice was amazing.

She missed her little shadow, her best friend. He'd gone to make war with her father at less than twelve years old. It was too young, but royalty grows up fast and everyone knew it.

Her magic tingled in her mind. She wanted those candied plums now. She could see them on a shelf in the larder, higher up than she could reach. She'd used her magic before to get at them. She felt like she should do so now.

Too far, she knew. She'd called for them from her room when she'd lived in the nursery once, and though she'd summoned them, the effort had knocked her out. It had also tripped every magic ward Nina and Shela had set up for her protection, bringing 300 armed guards and her mother to investigate with murder on their minds.

Shela had switched her until she bled for being so careless. Still, she'd been proud of what she'd done, almost a year ago.

Actually, she reasoned, she had no idea how far she was from home, and she'd become more powerful in a year. She *might* be able to summon sugared plums. She knew where they were, she knew what they looked like. A summoning required little more.

It wasn't like a transportation spell, where she moved her physical body to another place. She knew from personal experience that even moving through a wall was hard. She'd never actually moved more than a few feet and the last time had 'landed' six inches off of the ground, crashing surprisingly hard. Summoning brought something familiar to her – she knew the thing, she controlled the landing. It was a lot less difficult.

The more she thought about it, the more she wanted those candied plums, and the more she rationalized she should be able to do it.

So in the end, with the dusk settling in, her stomach growling and no sign yet of Hectaro, she called for them – those yummy plums that melted in her mouth, encased in a sealed glass jar with a metal ring locking down the glass top and a thin film of wax sealing in their freshness.

Her eyes unfocused, she saw the mason jar in her mind in the larder, imagined it down to a little bit of rust on the ring, and she willed it to her.

She felt a little tug on her finger ends, as if there were a spirit within her reaching out for the plums, and her body anchored her. The sensation felt familiar, although stronger than she remembered.

She bore down with her will, she called for the plums.

A white flash at the ends of her fingers left her seeing spots. As they cleared she felt before she saw the familiar feel of a mason jar in her hands. She smelled the wax seal, and she knew what it contained inside.

She couldn't be *too* far from home, a thought which comforted her more than the plums would, hungry as she was. She resolved to wait for Hectaro before she broke the seal, though.

He'd be proud of her for doing what she did.

***

He showed up in the beginning of the night, the red dusk settling to the west behind the rolling hills, painting the few clouds in the blackening sky. He'd run as far as he dared to the west, for want of a better direction, then he'd run back.

"Isn't that dangerous?" he asked her, as she broke the seal on the plums. "Couldn't you – I mean, isn't there a thing called 'the black mind?'"

The black mind happened to a wizard or a sorceress who cast a spell too powerful for her abilities. No one knew for sure what happened, but it would turn a person into a drooling lump unable to speak or react to the word around her, and it never went away.

The idea that he would interrogate her irritated Lee. He wasn't a sorceress; he didn't know anything about it. "I'm not going to get the black mind from summoning plums," she said. "If it didn't work it just wouldn't have worked. Nothing would have happened."

"How about noise – you know, another wizard knowing you're here?"

That was true. "I wish," she said. "Another wizard would save us."

Hectaro shook his head. "I don't know that," he said. "Neither do you. We could be in Volkhydro, we could be in Dorkan. Both places have wizards who hate your father. We could be in Andoron, and one of the tribes capturing the daughter of the head of the Wolf Rider tribe –"

"Alright!" Lee told him, exasperated. She's been very proud of herself and Hectaro was ruining it. He still wanted the plums, she noted. He'd even made her save four of them for D'leer when she woke up.

A stupid idea, she thought. She could always get more.

Who cares *what* Hectaro said? She was Lee Mordetur, daughter of the Emperor, and she did as she liked.

***

They fell asleep in the open, under the stars. She'd shed her dress and slept on top of it, two of her underskirts serving as a blanket. Hectaro saw her naked but she'd travelled with him before – Andaron women weren't shy of their bodies.

Hectaro hadn't looked twice at her, like a good Wolf Soldier. It was sort of disappointing, but she didn't lose sleep over it.

She awoke with the sun, the first thing to greet her bleary eyes being D'leer with her sword in its sheath over her shoulder, finishing off the last of the plums.

Lee sat up, holding her skirts to her breast. D'leer was squatting like a man, back on her heels, her knees apart. There was a trickle of purple juice running from the corner of her mouth to her chin.

"You had plums?" she asked Lee.

"Not anymore," the princess replied, somewhat dryly.

"Where did you keep them?"

Lee sighed and looked to her left where Hectaro still lay sleeping. He'd run a long way.

He'd been hungry.

She needed to put D'leer in her place, let her know she wasn't dealing with some defenseless girl but with an accomplished sorceress.

Having done it already, she held her hand out, she unfocused her eyes and she called for the plums. She knew it would appear in hand, she'd done it and she'd do it again.

This time it was different. She didn't prepare like she did last time. She had a general idea of what she wanted, she didn't focus like she should have.

She felt the same tugging at her fingers, but this time the pull felt stronger. She felt herself pulled out of her body and stretched out across the land, across the mountains to the east, past them to more plains, past them to a forest, and past the forest to Tren Bay.

She felt herself stretched, stretched, stretched – past the water to the land, across the land to the familiar walls of Galnesh Eldador, into the city, into the palace, into the kitchens.

She had the mason jar, and she snapped back faster than sound, faster than light, so fast she saw sun beams like spears crashing down around her as she flew past them.

The mason jar appeared with a loud *bang* and a blinding flash. Lee's skirts went flying and she rolled off of her place in the hollow, flying naked down the hill. The jar dropped to the ground and didn't break, landing in the pile of her dress. She pushed herself up to her hands and knees and fell back down to the ground.

She felt two hands on her, then tried to push them away and felt four. Her first thought was, "Great, now Hectaro was going to think he was right."

Then she had no thoughts, and consciousness left her.

***

She woke again with the sun off of the horizon. It must have been hours.

D'leer and Hectaro were standing over her. They'd eaten half of the plums.

Her stomach churned. She was sick and hungry at the same time. She'd done a stupid thing – she knew better.

It was Hectaro's fault. He shouldn't have questioned her. D'leer deserved some of the blame, too.

Tears welled up in her eyes as she realized how badly she wanted her mom. Why had both her parents left her alone to run the Empire? She was only *fourteen*. This wasn't fair.

"Are you well, your Highness?" Hectaro asked her, concern plain on his face.

They'd dressed her in her under skirts and a make-shift chemise D'leer must have tied together from another of her underskirts.

She sat up and reached out for the jar of plums. D'leer handed them to her without a word. She reached into the jar and fished one of the sticky plums out and devoured it, then another, then a third. She wanted to just upend the jar but she knew it wasn't proper.

"Highness?" Hectaro repeated.

She put the plums down, and she chewed, and she swallowed. She felt the sun on her face as she turned her face up, looked into D'leer's eyes and Hectaro's.

"I did another casting," she admitted. "I reached across the land, but this time I went with it. I saw the whole distance. I know where we are."

They stared down at her. She looked up at them.

"We're in Conflu," she informed them. "I'm sure of it – I saw."

They didn't say anything, digesting the reality of their situation. There was no nation with worse relations with the Eldadorian Empire than the Confluni. They'd even invaded Eldador this year.

Vedeen couldn't have put Lee in a worse situation if she'd turned her back over to the Trenboni.

Chapter Four

Underway

The region of Fovean on the planet named for the gods Earth and Water consisted of nine Fovean Nations, three of them ruled by kings and two ruled by Emperors: Eldador and Conflu.

The Confluni Emperor had been the only one before Lee's father had changed the nature of Eldador from a kingdom. He'd done this by establishing a tribe which he called the Wolf Rider Clan in the nation of Andoron and declaring them an Eldadorian protectorate.

Conflu had tried to invade Eldador three times, failing all three times in direct conflicts with Rancor Mordetur. As a Duke known as Lupus and as a member of a band of mercenaries known as the Daff Kanaar, he had invaded Conflu in a rather famous event known as the Battle of Tamaran Glen, where 100 Wolf Soldiers leading a few thousand Daff Kanaari warriors had defeated more than five times their number in Confluni warriors. Lee had been taught this offense had prompted the bad relations between the two empires. Conflu maintained a thick system of patrols throughout its borders and murdered *anyone* they caught entering the country.

The slight her father had delivered to them was unforgivable. It would fulfill every fantasy the Confluni Emperor had ever enjoyed, to have the daughter of his greatest enemy in his hands.

"Are you sure?" Hectaro asked her. D'leer was already nodding.

"If she's not, I am," she said. Hectaro took a step back to regard her, and Lee fished another plum out of the jar.

"We're in Destruction's month, but it's hot at night," she said. "That means we're not in the north, someplace like Volkhydro. These are hills, not flat plains, so we can't be in Andoron. I look to the east and I see what I think are mountains, though, and there are no mountains to the east of anywhere in Eldador. That only leaves one place."

"But Conflu is heavily wooded," Hectaro argued. The sweet taste of the sugared plum exploded in Lee's mouth. "There's nothing here – there's not a tree for daheeri."

"I don't see how every single bit of Conflu could be wooded," D'leer said, frowning. There was still a brown discoloration at the tear in her uniform at her hip, Lee noted. She'd drawn out what blood she could but magic didn't replace a good washing, and blood was hard to get out of thick cotton.

"No one we know has been deep into Conflu, other than her father," D'leer continued, pointing at Lee. "Even he found only a glen, not wide, rolling hills. We're not just in Conflu, we're *deep* in Conflu, Wolf Soldier. We're going to be walking for a long time."

"And hiding for most of it," Lee said. "As soon as anyone sees us, they're going to know we're not from here."

The Confluni were, as far as anyone knew, of the race of Men, but shorter than Eldadorians, less burly than Volkhydrans, and while darker skinned than either, not reddish like Andarons or brown like Toorians, but more yellowish, with slanted eyes, usually brown, and tending to have black or grey hair.

By treaty all Fovean nations were limited to an army of no larger than 20,000 warriors. The Eldadorians exceeded the limit five times, and the Confluni had fielded armies as large as 65,000 on more than one occasion prior to the Mordeturs coming to power. No one knew how vast their nation was, and then no one knew the extent of their armies.

"OK," D'leer said, taking three steps away and facing both of them. "We need to start moving east, and we need to keep low and out of sight. We'll move for as long as we can into the night, and then sleep and adjust to a night schedule, and keep out of sight in the day."

"And who," Lee asked, standing, trying not to feel ridiculous in her one skirt and manufactured top, "do you think you are, to be telling *me* to do *anything*?"

D'leer rolled her Uman eyes. She'd tied her long green hair back behind her head in a pony tail accentuating her pointed ears and high cheek bones.

"Lee," she said, "when we're back in Galnesh Eldador, *if* we make it that far, you can go back to –"

Lee called the white light and held her left hand out between her and the Uman Wolf Soldier. Hectaro pulled his sword from its sheath and held it in both hands between him and D'leer, taking on a fighting crouch and putting his feet at shoulder width apart.

Lee already knew what D'leer would say. Be a good little princess and listen to the grownups. We'll take care of you.

"You're a traitor, D'leer," she said. The Uman didn't reach for her sword, but straightened and put her hands on her hips. Uman women tended to be willowy but Uman had the body of a woman of the race of Man, with full hips and breasts. Lee knew she never wanted for suitors and prided herself on being a match for any male.

"You turned on me in favor of Angron Aurelias," Lee said. "I saved you, and as far as you're concerned you owe your life to me, but don't think I've forgotten for a second you're a traitor to the Empire, to the oath you made to my father, and to your Wolf Soldier command."

Lee knew what her words meant, and she knew how they stung. The Wolf Soldiers were the most feared fighting force Fovea had ever seen. Its members, the Pack, were composed entirely of people on their second chance – criminals and outcasts, persons who had lost life's game. The Pack was their second chance, and they were fiercely loyal to the Mordetur family.

There had been very few traitors in their ranks, and their fates were horror stories.

"I'm the most experienced warrior and leader –" D'leer began.

The white light turned red. Lee let it drip little sparks. It was a magical effect her mother had taught her by accident a year ago, when she'd caught a servant flirting with the Emperor.

"I don't trust you," Lee said. "You can stay with us, and you may fight for us, but I don't trust you, D'leer, and you're not telling me what to do.

"I saved you, but give me a reason and I'll send you back to your god."

D'leer looked the princess in the eye, searched her face, then nodded. Likely she was already planning how she'd leave them, Lee decided, but until she did she'd make good use of D'leer.

The Uman probably had her reasons for her betrayal, and she probably thought them good ones, but Lee couldn't worry about D'leer's past now. Her mother had taught her as part of her becoming a sorceress to take the world as it was, not as she would have it. People did things. Events happened. You couldn't wish them away, you can only build on them or step past them as you moved forward.

"We *will* start moving east," Lee informed them, letting her hand go dark. Hectaro straightened but left his sword out. A gentle breeze caught Lee's and D'leer's hair.

"D'leer, you'll take point," she said. "You're the most experienced – we'll use that. We'll follow half a daheer behind you. You're to make no contact. If you see signs of the Confluni, you'll make a fist over your head and lay down. If you're safe you'll wait for us to catch up to you, otherwise you'll retreat to the north. We'll go south and meet you back to the west."

D'leer nodded. Without another word she took off to the east at a jog. Hectaro watched her go for a while, then turned his attention back to Lee.

"Where did you learn all of that?" he asked.

"My father's advisors drill my brother and I all the time," she said. She squatted down and started folding up her dress. She didn't want to wear it but she didn't want to waste it, either. There was always a good use for cloth.

She also didn't want Hectaro to see her cry. This was too much. Yes, her father's advisors had drilled this sort of knowledge into her, but she'd never expected to *use* it. She never thought she'd be on the other side of Fovea, surrounded by her enemies. She never thought she'd be doing something like this at all.

A few months ago she'd been playing dolls with her younger brother and sister, and complaining they didn't do it right.

Times changed.

***

They jogged across the plains. Lee hadn't thought to create a signal for D'leer to tell her to stop, and so the Uman woman set a punishing pace for them to follow. More than once they lost all sight of her, only to find her again either sitting on the top of a hill or resting in the sun. By the time the sun was high in the sky, Lee's feet were starting to blister and her stomach was growling.

By then her palace slippers were in tatters.

"We have to stop," Hectaro informed her.

"I'll – I'll – I'll be fine," Lee panted.

"You aren't fine," he informed her, and stopped. She almost fell beside him. "You need shoes for this sort of thing. You won't do us any good if you cripple yourself and we have to carry you."

"I can wrap my feet in cloth from my dress," she said. "That should last a while, and I have a lot. Eventually we'll find – "

But Hectaro shook his head. "Can't you do with some of your clothes what you did with the plums?" he asked.

Lee sighed. Stupid, she thought. Of *course* she could summon them. She knew her closet intimately. She had a tough set of riding boots in the back of her armoire, to the right hand side, with a brass buckle on a shelf above them. They sat on a tough pair of pants for riding and a cloak.

She unfocused her eyes. She imagined the clothes exactly as she'd left them. She remembered how the fold lay against the back of the armoire, that the toes of the boots were pointed toward her.

She remembered the cost of failure but she drove it out of her mind. She could do this.

She asserted her will. She wasn't caught only half way prepared this time. There was a little flash in front of her, and there sat her clothes as she remembered them.

She didn't have a proper shirt yet, but this would make moving a *lot* easier.

Hectaro politely turned his back to her. She stepped into the pants under her skirt and then shed the article. She ripped several strips from the hem of her skirt and she wrapped her feet in them, and then she slid her foot into her boot.

She withdrew it immediately as she found something in there that didn't belong. Hectaro still watching the horizon, she reached into her boot and pulled out a crumpled piece of parchment.

It read, "Wouldn't you also like to have your horse?"

It was signed, "G."

Chapter Five

More Help

The day wore on, the daheeri passed under their feet. Lee's boots made travel less of a misery to her, and the wrappings she'd made for herself did even more.

The sun beat down and the flowers smelled fresh – it wasn't a bad place for a run if you weren't in the homeland of your most dire enemy.

They saw game once in a while – a kind of antelope by the look of it, wild on the plain. The animals seemed both curious and shy, not running at the site of them, but not letting them come close, either. D'leer had thrown a dagger at one and missed it. She hadn't gotten close enough for her sword.

She was starving but she'd already grown tired of sugared plums. They made for a sweet reward when stolen from the larder, not so appetizing as a staple.

When the sun set D'leer called a halt on her own. Hectaro and Lee were too exhausted to argue with her.

"We can eat grass," she said. "There's nutrition in it. Certainly it's better than nothing."

"Is there any other sort of food you know of and can call to you?" Hectaro asked her, almost pleading.

Lee shook her head. "The larder is full all of the time," she said, "but that doesn't mean I know what's in it. My brother and I used to steal the plums, so I knew where they were kept. There was bread in there, hams, everything we liked to eat, but the kitchen staff moves it all around as they need it."

D'leer nodded, Hectaro after her. The message from 'G' recurred to her.

Yes, she thought. She *would* like to have her horse. Especially Hectaro's *Bastard,* a stallion from the line of her father's horse *Blizzard*, a grey fast enough to run down a gazelle and tough enough to do it all day.

With horses they'd cut their travel down to a fraction of the time, and as far as she knew the Confluni didn't ride. Their chances were much better on horseback.

"Well, there's worms and bugs in the ground, too," D'leer was saying.

As if Lee needed another argument.

Without a word of explanation she unfocused her eyes. The dusk was on them and the other two didn't immediately realize what she was doing. She knew the paddock where her own mare, *Singer*, was kept. She'd be in now. The mares grazed the outer pastures during the day, some stallions and the geldings at night. Bastard wouldn't be turned out with the bachelor herd for fear he'd kill the other stallions, and because no one but Hectaro could handle him.

The timing couldn't be better. She knew Bastard almost as well as she knew Singer. She knew where they'd be. She envisioned them in her mind.

This was no jar of plums. The horses weighed more than a dozen full-grown Men. Even though she knew where they were and what they looked like, Singer down to the length of her tail, she'd never done this with so much mass.

She risked the black mind. She'd already decided she'd take the chance. She couldn't keep finding them food as she had – they couldn't keep moving without it. She wasn't about to eat grass and bugs.

She felt the horses with her mind. She sensed their startled reaction to this intrusion – she knew something of their minds. She made a connection, she felt her being streeeeeeetch out of her body, back across the plains, back across the mountains, the forest, the Bay, the land of Eldador and into Galnesh Eldador and the palace.

The horses weren't jars, they were living things. They reacted as living things – with fear. They resisted.

She wasn't ready for their resistance.

She pulled back, they came with her, kicking and rearing, calling out for the assistance of the herd. Together they snapped back across the distance from Eldador to Conflu.

Along the way she saw a city to her east this time, and a pass through the mountains. She couldn't tell if there were people there, but she couldn't imagine why there wouldn't be.

She fell back onto her butt as the two terrified horses appeared before her. Her chestnut mare reared and pawed the air, the grey stallion Bastard spun on his front hooves, kicking out at nothing, as if the world offended him and he'd kill it.

Darkness washed over her like a wave. She fell back sick to her stomach, hearing the horses neighing and Hectaro bellowing, vaguely aware when D'leer leapt over her to put her body between hers and the horses.

***

She woke with the sun on her face, starving. She blinked at the pain of the light in her eyes. She smelled horse manure mixed with crushed grass and something cooking.

In the back of her mind, she knew she'd pushed herself too far. She'd tried to do too much, and she hadn't been ready. Mixed with this admission came the exultation that she'd *done* it – she'd done magic any adult would have been proud of.

She'd probably saved them.

"You're awake," she heard Hectaro inform her.

She blinked again and pushed herself up onto her elbows. Hectaro was standing, holding his horse Bastard's head. D'leer and Singer were nowhere to be seen.

She scanned the horizon – the same hills she remembered. The mountains to the east were more prominent now.

"Where?" she asked. "I thought – I brought... Where?"

Where is D'leer? Where is her horse? Her mind was swimming – she couldn't form the words.

"D'leer took your horse to scout," Hectaro said. "Bastard wouldn't let her on him, and I wasn't about to leave her here with you alone."

Lee didn't like someone else riding her horse, but she didn't disagree with Hectaro's logic, either. D'leer couldn't be trusted. If she had to be left alone with a horse, she couldn't be left alone with a helpless princess as well.

Lee just hoped she'd come back.

"You summoned these," Hectaro said. He pronounced it as a statement, not a question.

She nodded. Her heart constricted just a little, though she didn't know why. She didn't answer to Hectaro. In fact, he answered to her, as the son of a Duke and as a Wolf Soldier.

"We thought you had the black mind," he informed her. His face sat dead serious, the beautiful brown eyes flat. "It took us hours to catch the horses. If not for D'leer, one would have trampled you."

"OK," Lee said. She knew she'd done too much. She didn't need to hear about it from Hectaro.

"If we'd have had some warning, we might have helped you," he said.

"You can't help me," Lee answered him.

"We might have protected you," he pressed her.

"I don't need your permission," she countered him.

"War's Beard, Lee!" he swore at her. She stiffened, startled, sitting on the ground. She'd have stood but she didn't trust her legs yet.

"You're not in this alone," he informed her. "We have to do this all together. You, me, even D'leer – we can't afford to lose you, Lee. You can't just put yourself in such danger without consulting us."

On the one hand she felt ashamed of herself – Hectaro was right. Her magic would be essential to their success and if she'd failed she could have robbed them of it. On the other hand, she reminded herself who she was, and what position she was in. As she'd been educated by her father's advisors, command couldn't be maintained by an unsure leader. She couldn't second guess herself and she couldn't let Hectaro do it for her.

She needed to lead. She'd made her decision, conversation over.

"We needed the horses," she informed him. "We're using them now. We can use them to travel and to hunt. In fact, I'm hungry. Why don't you get on Bastard and run us down a gazelle?"

Hectaro straightened. "You're not listening," he informed her.

"It isn't my job to listen," she said. "I'm not your servant; I'm not in your command. I am Princess Lee Mordetur, daughter of the Emperor of Eldador, and you're a Wolf Soldier assigned to my protection. Is that clear?"

Hectaro's lip curled a little but he straightened. "It is," he informed her.

"You have your orders," she said. "Carry them out."

He made a fist over his heart in salute to her, then turned on one heel and took Bastard by the mane. He led the stallion to a natural depression in the hand, then bounced once and dragged himself up onto the horse's back, still holding on to the mane. He touched his heels to the stallion's ribs and the huge stallion, seventeen hands tall at the withers with a huge, arched neck, a giant round cheek and a tiny nose, took off at a trot.

Riding bareback wasn't hard if the horse was stable. At six years old, Bastard was well broken and Lee had no doubt Hectaro had ridden him without a saddle.

In this terrain it would still be dangerous, and in fact it made sense while she was scouting, D'leer would be hunting as well. She hadn't thought to ask.

Fine – she might have made a mistake. It wasn't her fault, she assured herself. She'd been put under a lot of pressure, and she was doing the best she could.

She'd gotten them horses. When she had rested and eaten, she'd get them saddles.

She watched Hectaro ride Bastard over one hill, disappear over its crest and then appear atop another. He'd be grateful for what she'd done, once he'd seen her do it.

Chapter Six

Revisiting Conflu

Lee's father had told her once, "*Food tastes better when you are starving.*" If you want to try something new, fast for a day, *then* try it.

She'd fasted for more than a day and she'd been casting spells like an Aschire fires arrows, and the roasted gazelle tasted so amazing to her, Lee could hardly believe it.

Hectaro had run it down from Bastard's back. D'leer had come back with a bundle of dry wood in hope of him doing just that. They claimed their plan had been to use the horses to hunt all along, but they'd wanted to take a wider look at the periphery first and make sure a camp fire wouldn't bring a horde of Confluni National Guard.

They found nothing. They returned and they dressed the gazelle, spitted it and roasted it over a low fire, keeping the smoke low in case they'd missed someone. D'leer handled the cooking while Hectaro checked the horses.

He'd cleaned their hooves and braided a rope from Lee's shredded dress, creating a simple hobble for each. He rubbed them down as best he could and he returned to the fire, saying nothing until they ate.

"I had another look over the land between here and home," Lee informed them, finally.

Both Wolf Soldiers regarded her, both eating, saying nothing. D'leer had cut long strip steaks from the gazelle, then moved the whole carcass to the side of the fire where the heat would dry it. She'd prepare jerked meat from it tonight and they'd eat for days.

Lee sighed. Her chin, neck and hands were covered with grease from the meat. Her stomach growled from the shock of the meal after a cross between sugar plums and nothing. Hectaro had found water but they had nothing to carry it in. They'd stretch the skin from the gazelle and make water skins. The animal's bladder could be used for carrying water as well.

"There's a city to the east," she said, not looking at either of them, focusing on the fire. "It's huge, and right up against a mountain range the size of the Iron Mountains. There's a road through the mountains. I couldn't see people, but that doesn't mean there were none."

Hectaro kept his face pointed at Lee but kept looking sideways at D'leer. D'leer had been his sergeant – he was used to getting guidance from her. He appeared to be looking for her guidance now.

Lee might have made a mistake in her treatment of him. She might have sent him right to D'leer's side. If that were true, she might have really endangered herself.

It was hard to know what to do – even moment to moment.

"We're right at the center of the range," she said. "Past it, there's the Confluni forests and then Tren Bay. We might make it across the range through the road I saw, but I don't see how we'll do it without attracting attention to ourselves. It would take us a month or more to travel around the mountain range, and then I don't know if we'd be any safer."

"So you know a little more," D'leer said, "but you don't know enough to make a decision."

Lee considered that.

"How can you do this?" Hectaro asked her. "Your mother can't do this sort of magic – she couldn't have taught you."

"You have no idea what my mother can do," Lee said to him.

"But she can't do that," D'leer reaffirmed. "I've campaigned with your mother – there have been times when we needed a skill like this. She can't do it."

Lee didn't have a lot to say about that.

She sighed.

"It's different," she informed them, finally. She could tell she had their attention without looking at them. "Sorcery isn't wizardry – it's different. They do things based on spells and formulas, we do what we do from our hearts, from the elements, from the gifts of gods. My mother is the waking representation of the god Power, and what he allows her is based on his needs as well as hers.

"I'm not sure of my god or goddess yet," Lee informed them. "While I'm gifted, we don't think it's by Power, so my magic isn't like my mother's."

"I didn't know this," D'leer admitted.

"No one knows this," Lee informed them. "Almost no one. They don't need to.

"But Hectaro says we need to work together, which means you need to," she continued. She finally looked up at each of them and met their eyes.

"I don't know for sure how I can do what I do," she said. "I know I used a *lot* of power. When it was easy, like with the plums, I could just... *do* it. When it was harder, it was like I was dragged there and then snapped back. I could see along the way."

"So you could do it again," D'leer said.

Lee shook her head. "I almost couldn't do it with the horses," she said. "I risked the black mind. I don't think I was supposed to be able to do what I did, and I don't think I'm supposed to be doing it the *way* I did.

"My mother would know," she concluded. "I really miss her."

Missing her mother was hard to admit to and she couldn't be sure she should have. No taking it back now. None of this was fair.

D'leer and Hectaro were both nodding and doing the frown adults sometimes did around her when she met some new goal. She didn't understand it. She needed to take charge back, that much she knew.

"The horses must be tired," she said. "It's dangerous to ride them at night when they can step in a hole and break a leg. We'll get up with the sun and travel east. We'll see how close we can get to that city, and then we'll see if we can find the road. If not, we'll decide together if we go north or south."

"I think south," Hectaro offered immediately. "We know –"

"We don't know," D'leer interrupted him. Both heads turned to her. "We don't know anything. We're deep in Conflu and we didn't even know that Conflu was deep. Conflu might be even larger than Eldador and no one knew it. This changes everything we know about Fovea."

"I don't see how –" Lee began, but D'leer wasn't finished.

"If Conflu is vast," she said, "and is older than Eldador, why aren't *they* the ones who rule Fovea? Clearly they want to. They've been at war with almost everyone. They've fielded giant armies.

"We have to ask ourselves, 'What's going on?'"

***

They went to sleep, they woke with the dawn, they had a problem right away.

"It makes more sense," D'leer protested.

Lee shook her head.

They had three riders, they had two horses. The larger and more powerful of them was Bastard.

Bastard should ride two, and Singer one. In fact, Singer wasn't strong enough to ride two all day, and they'd be going a long way.

But Lee just didn't want the Uman whore to have her legs wrapped around Hectaro all day. D'leer should walk, but she would slow them down. It made it pointless, in fact, to have the horses.

So it was an impossible situation.

"I'm not walking and I can't ride with you," D'leer said.

Hectaro started grinning and made everything worse. Lee felt her face turn red. She looked away and she heard Hectaro pull himself up on to Bastard's back.

She heard D'leer leap up after him.

It was stupid. She knew it, but it made her angry. This gave them something on her, which she didn't like. She led them this way.

"We ride," she said, gruffly, and she heard her voice catch. She touched her heels to Singer's ribs as she took the horse's mane in her hand. Singer trotted off and Bastard took up after her.

If she stayed ahead, at least she didn't have to look at them.

They crossed the daheeri more rapidly on horseback. The changes in the terrain came more quickly. There were long, flat gullies among the hills which must become washes when it rained. The horses took them at a canter. There were rough, loosely graveled hills that the horses had a hard time scrambling up onto. Both of them were shod, but shoes could be a blessing now and a curse later. In a few weeks those shoes were going to have to be changed, and there probably weren't a lot of proper blacksmiths in Conflu who traded in horses.

Where the people didn't ride.

The mountains kept growing in the East. Three days after they'd summoned their horses, they saw signs of the first cities.

There were outlying farms, wide marshes growing rice, surrounded by bogs with some sort of red berry and, farther out, other vegetables in neat squares. She didn't see corn but she saw melons, tomatoes, different sorts of beans. The more they looked, the more they saw.

People didn't seem to move into or out of the city much. There were thousands in the vast fields. Lee recognized the Confluni.

She could have lived with being wrong.

"What now?" Hectaro asked her.

"We watch?" D'leer said.

Sitting and watching didn't seem like a good idea to Lee. They needed to get moving. They needed to hunt again soon, and there wouldn't be much around a city like this.

"What?" Hectaro questioned her. "Why?"

D'leer pointed at the city. "We don't know anything about those people," she said, "but they don't seem to be doing anything other than farming. I didn't see one patrol. If they just come out, farm and go back, then we can bypass them. Farmers aren't curious about much. We'll learn more and be safer if we take a day and see what we're about."

D'leer's logic made tremendous good sense to Lee, which aggravated her, because it should have been her idea. D'leer was *not* taking over this mission. She was *not* the leader.

"Is that your recommendation, then, D'leer?" Lee asked her.

Hectaro suppressed a smile and looked away, and Lee didn't miss it. D'leer tried not to roll her eyes.

"Yes, of course, your Highness," she said, finally. She was making it very clear how she felt.

Lee nodded. "We can wait a day," she said.

"We need more than – " D'leer began.

"A day," she repeated. "We'll move the horses back a daheer, behind that last bank of hills. Farmers aren't curious but their children are.

"You scout on foot. Take a skin and some jerked meat. Keep your greys on but lose the tunic – everyone knows the symbol on them means."

D'leer turned to Hectaro for support.

"You heard her," he said.

"Hectaro, this is *serious*," she said.

Lee knew where *that* would end up. It infuriated her.

"Would you rather head out on your own?" Lee asked her.

D'leer raised an eyebrow and crossed her arms under her breasts.

"I lead here," Lee said. She'd been counseled against this in her training. The leader who had to proclaim her leadership lost face for her troops, but Lee couldn't think of any other way.

"You've already betrayed your vows, D'leer," she said. "You're lucky I let you live. You've been useful so I've kept you. Start defying me now and you can go on your own way, no horse, no food."

D'leer looked to Hectaro again for support.

He crossed his arms like she had and put his feet apart, at shoulder width. Not only would he support her, he'd fight.

Now it was Lee smiling.

"Your will, your Highness," D'leer said. She took a skin and a hand full of jerked meat, and she took off at a trot. Lee took a hand full of Singer's mane and Hectaro took Bastard's and they both mounted. She was getting used to doing this with no saddle.

She'd needed to rely on Hectaro. Her father or her mother would have taken command and kept it on the strength of their personality.

But maybe leading this way was good, too.

Chapter Seven

Woman in Charge

Lee and Hectaro retreated to a gulley where the horses had liked to run. Lee wanted to set up camp there but Hectaro argued there were enough clouds in the sky where it might rain, and instead they found another hollow in another hill, and set themselves up there.

They ate and they rested until the sun set. Hectaro walked out to the top of the highest of the hills several times, taking long minutes to search the horizon before returning to her. They cleaned the horses' hooves and rubbed them down.

They did things to take up time, but it was too tense to rest and to dangerous not to.

"She'll be ok," Lee informed him, returning as the sun set in his eyes.

"You hope," he countered.

The response surprised her. Hectaro let his opinion be known but he usually didn't voice his displeasure to her. True, they were alone, but there were protocols.

"I wonder if you even understand what you told her to do?" he continued.

She frowned. "She's doing recon," she said. "She's trained to do that, you know."

Hectaro seated himself by the entrance to the hollow in the hill. He put his back against the hill itself and looked up at her, standing in front of him.

"She's doing recon, but she doesn't have the time to do it right," he said. "She's got to cover as many daheeri as she could run in a day, in less than a day, and she's got to stay hidden while she does it. You see a city against the mountains with fields, and you think, 'Check out the terrain.'

"She sees a half circle she has to run twice, and anywhere along it she might find the one person who will see her and run screaming to the city guard."

Lee hadn't thought of it that way at all. Recon was something you told your soldiers to do if you were a smart commander. They went out and they did it, simple as ordered.

It was dangerous, but being a Wolf Soldier was dangerous. If you were afraid, you shouldn't be a Wolf Soldier.

She said as much.

Hectaro shook his head. "A Wolf Soldier is a part of the Pack," he said. "We're alone. If there were a thousand of us, or one hundred, or a squad, we'd work together. We'd send some out and keep some here to watch you.

"But there's two, there's me and her, and she knows we can't trust her. She betrayed us and you don't even care why. You send her out like this and she has to think it's because you don't care if she dies. When you start treating your people like they're expendable, they start wondering why they're staying around."

Lee's first reaction found this sort of insolence inexcusable, but she tried to make herself see beyond her simple need to be in charge. Hectaro had proven himself a loyal warrior and a confidant – he tried to be both now. She swallowed some of the anger this made her feel, but she couldn't swallow all of it.

"I hear your complaint, Wolf Soldier," she said, and she knew the straight, thin line of her lips spoke of her anger, "and maybe what I'm doing seems harsh to you.

"But if the truth has to be known, then yes, if I have to lose one of you, then I'm going to lose her if I can help it. She's a traitor, Hectaro. She was going to get you killed and turn me over to Angron Aurelias.

Do you know what Angron Aurelias would *do* to me to get my father under control?"

She was gratified when Hectaro didn't seem to have an answer for her question.

"I don't know if your father educated you in this, but Uman-Chi like Angron Aurelias see the race of Men as being more animal than anything else. I wasn't looking forward to being raped. I wasn't looking forward to having my fingers or my toes cut off and sent to my mother. I wasn't looking forward to being tied naked to the outside of some tower or flying bridge in Outpost IX when my father laid siege to the city, and I *really* wasn't looking forward to having my gut opened as a lesson to him when he stormed the city!"

Hectaro looked shocked, which she found gratifying, too. Her mother had had this talk with her. Girls among the Andarons were captured as a point of honor among the tribes – the people who'd raised Shela had been as frank with her as the daughter of a powerful chieftain.

Shela hadn't, as her father said, 'pulled any punches,' and Lee didn't now.

"So if you don't think I'm being as nice as I might be with D'leer, Wolf Soldier, then *you* keep that in your fucking pack, and you do your *fucking* job!"

That part was a direct quote from her father but it felt good to say it. Her mother would have slapped her mouth dry, but she wasn't here.

Hectaro nodded and looked away. He'd made a point here, but she had to.

She crawled into the hollow and lay down on the remains of her palace dress, which was getting pretty ragged.

Tomorrow, she was getting them their saddles.

***

The dawn came early. She'd rested well. Hectaro looked like he'd stayed up all night, and it occurred to her he might have.

She hadn't offered to take any part of the watch, but she'd assumed D'leer and Hectaro had divided it. D'leer, apparently, hadn't come back.

"I want to take Bastard out –" Hectaro began.

Lee shook her head. "No."

"She might be in trouble," he argued.

"Then she's in trouble," Lee said. "If she can't handle it, you can't."

That shut him down.

"Take some sleep," she ordered him. "I left the bedding in there. I'll keep watch."

He looked into the hollow and looked to the east where the sun was rising, and where D'leer was either watching Confluni or being killed by them.

"Now, Wolf Soldier," she informed him.

He nodded and he pulled off his tunic, then the leather breast guard underneath it. He stripped off the grey shirt and pants, leaving him in his leather breach clout.

Lee looked away. Old feelings rose in her. Hectaro had been her first crush. He was beyond handsome, and campaigning as they were had left him all muscle and sweat.

Mother would have told her just to take him from one side of her mouth, and killed him herself from the other. Lee suppressed a grin.

"What?" Hectaro asked her, having caught her checking him out, no doubt.

"D'leer's going to think we slept together," Lee lied.

Hectaro shook his head and crawled into the bedding. "She's not the jealous kind," he told her from within the hollow.

Jealous of what? Lee couldn't help wondering.

***

The sun was at its highest point in the sky when D'leer returned. Hectaro was snoring away in the hollow.

The horses had cropped a wide space of grass clear. If someone came looking for evidence they weren't going to have a hard time finding it, Lee had been thinking.

D'leer took a look around her and she clearly felt the same way. "You shouldn't have stayed so long in the same place," she informed Lee, simply.

Lee shook her head. "There was more danger in moving," she said.

D'leer shrugged.

"Report, Wolf Soldier," Lee said, parroting her father again.

D'leer smiled and looked down. She pulled two pieces of jerked meat from her belt pouch and offered Lee one. She took it. Both took a bite and chewed.

"They're Confluni farmers," she said, around a mouth full of meat, "but we knew that. They don't have out-buildings or guards or patrols. We could stay here a year and we'd probably not be found."

Lee somehow doubted the time frame but didn't say anything.

"I found that road through the mountains," she continued, sitting. She turned her face up to the sun and let it shine on her, closing her wild Uman eyes. "Didn't see anyone on it, coming down it or going up it. I think they use this city to grow food and only come here when they want to gather it, but that's a guess and I can't swear to it. I don't know what day this is, so I don't know if maybe this is some holy day when they don't travel."

"Were they working?" Lee asked.

D'leer opened one eye, regarded her and closed it. "Farmers work every day," she said, "but yeah, I don't think it's a holy day, either. I think they just don't use that road unless they need to."

"So we might travel it," Lee said.

D'leer sighed and laid back. The woman was worn out, but her condition wasn't the point of this.

A Wolf Soldier should be giving her report at attention. D'leer was being defiant. If Lee pushed her, D'leer would be thinking Lee wasn't secure in her command, and if not, then she was getting away with this. Either way, Lee lost.

"You forget how to give a report, Wolf Solider?" Lee challenged her.

"No, ma'am," she said. "But you made it pretty clear I betrayed the Pack, so I have to wonder if I'm still a Wolf Soldier."

Was she doing all of this to get back to her execution on time, she meant.

"You had a reason for what you did?" Lee informed her.

D'leer opened one eye and regarded her.

As a woman, D'leer had to know what would have been in store for Lee.

"You're going to tell me what you did and why, when you're ready," Lee said. "For where we are, I have to accept that.

"Until then you're a Wolf Soldier, unless you don't think you can hack it anymore."

That got her. D'leer pulled herself up onto her feet.

"I didn't have much time," D'leer said, "but I don't think they use that road much. I didn't see fresh tracks on it, but there was a pretty deep path, complete with wagon grooves, from it down to the city. I think they caravan in during the harvest, which means we have *weeks* to use it."

Lee nodded. "Good report, Wolf Soldier," she said. "Hectaro's in the hollow. Go sleep, and I'll wake him in a few hours. He can run down another gazelle, and we'll jerk the meat and pack as much natural grain and hay as we can, then we'll cross the mountains tomorrow night."

"Yes, Lee," D'leer said.

Wolf Soldiers all called her father 'Lupus.' Her father was unique – he let his people call him by his nick name, and it became his title to them. That had saved his life once.

When her brother had taken command of a troop of Wolf Soldiers, when she and her sister and her mother and Hectaro had been captured by Bounty Hunters, the Wolf Soldiers had called him, "Vulpe" to show their respect. It was a big deal.

This was a big deal. Lee smiled.

D'leer made a fist over her heart, dropped her hand, and then turned on her heel and went into the hollow.

Lee felt pretty good about herself, until she realized D'leer must have had some energy left, based on what she was doing in the hollow with Hectaro.

Chapter Eight

More and Even Better

Lee spent the late morning and the early afternoon pouting. She tried to think of a better term for it but there wasn't one. She couldn't *believe* they would do that with her *right there*. D'leer had done it to get even but Hectaro must have just not cared. She was really starting to like him again, too.

She thought it might be good to go for a ride and clear her head, but she needed to be responsible and stand guard. She spent some time pulling mats out of the horses' manes and tails. Bastard actually surprised her by letting her curry him with one of Hectaro's daggers.

She had them all but gleaming when Hectaro rousted himself out of the hollow.

"Hello," he mumbled.

She didn't answer.

He went into their supplies and found the last hand full of jerked meat. He stuffed half of it into his mouth and chewed, offering the rest to her in his open hand.

Like a dog. Like a pet. Like the princess he kept around. "You eat it," she said. "You're going to go out and run down another gazelle. We're heading into the mountains tomorrow night."

He nodded. He took his time chewing, swallowed, and then took the rest of the jerked meat into his mouth and started again.

"He let you curry him," he noted.

This was impossible!

He picked the stallion's hooves up one-by-one and cleaned them with his dagger. He scraped the area around the frog white and then cut a little flare away from the insides. He checked the shoes for tightness and seemed to be ok with what he found.

"I'll be gone past dusk," he said. "They come out as the sun goes down so I'll need to wait, then I'll dress it and we'll be back."

She nodded. "Try to get one with horns," she said.

He regarded her. "Why?"

"Because I told you to, alright?" she snapped at him. "I need it."

He shrugged. "If I can," he said. "The ones with horns are dangerous. I don't want to risk Bastard."

"Wait a minute," she said.

She unfocused her eyes. She knew the tack room in the royal stables intimately. She knew where they kept their saddles, and she knew Hectaro's. It was the obvious property of a royal – silver trimmed, padded seat, high cantle and silver-tooled stirrups. She knew the flashing on the side, the pickups on the bridle. He always looped the bit and bridle over the pommel. She knew he preferred a snaffle, a jointed bit.

She saw it all in her mind, and she called for the saddle.

This time it was easy, almost a relief after the effort of the horses. The saddle, the bit and the bridle just dropped into her hands. She grunted a little at the weight – this was a lancer's saddle, designed to keep a warrior from being knocked back out of the seat and off of the back of the horse. She tried to toss it to a surprised Hectaro but ended up throwing it at his feet.

"There," she said.

"Was it – was that… are you ok?" he managed.

She shrugged. "It was easy this time," she said.

"Did you travel all the way to Eldador this time?"

"No," she said. "I only do that when it's hard."

"Maybe if you focused on just the seeing, you could," Hectaro said.

She frowned and shook her head. He shrugged and squatted down to pick up his saddle.

"There's no blanket," he told her.

"What?"

"No blanket," he said. "You can't just put the saddle on the horse's back – you need a pad."

He was right, of course. The problem was there was a stack of pads in the stable, and it was always different. You use one, it absorbed the horse's sweat, you hung it up to dry and took another as you needed it. She didn't have a favorite and she really didn't care about which one she took. They all looked different, designed at the whim of the person who made it, but none of them stood out in her mind.

Without a blanket, the saddle was worse than useless, and they couldn't just use cloth from her dress. The blanket needed not to wrinkle, to help fit the horse's back to the saddle's interior.

She sighed. This was going to hurt.

"You can't just call for any one blanket, can you?" he asked her.

"No," she informed him.

"Can you call the whole pile?" he asked.

She squinted at him. "What?"

"You don't know what each blanket looks like, but you know what the whole pile looks like, don't you?"

Lee had to recognize such a good idea. Thing was – she didn't need the whole pile.

Then again – if things started turning up missing, someone was going to start asking why, and there were some excellent wizards among her father's Wolf Soldier guard.

She unfocused her eyes.

This time as she called for the blankets, as her being wanted to pull out of her body, she let it go a little farther. She separated her being from her *self*, and she traveled down along the path of the spell.

She travelled across the city, she moved down the pass. She could see there was no one on it. There were places every few daheeri where water was collected. Someone maintained this place, but they didn't use it much.

As she was studying this, the pile of blankets seemed to come flying out of the east. It crashed into her and knocked her all of the way back to her actual body.

A moment later she went flying backwards and a pile of blankets flew all over the place. One of them covered her face, reeking of horse.

"Wow," Hectaro said. She couldn't see where he was.

"That worked, huh?"

She felt his hands on her and pushed him away. She got up on her own, picked up a blanket and tossed it to him.

"Try that one," she said.

***

Hectaro rode off, but not before she pulled another message off of the fleece lining connected to his saddle's inside. The lining was common with saddles, the message not so much.

It read, "You'll need a blanket." It was signed, 'G'. Whoever sent this now thought she was following her instructions.

So someone knew what she was doing. There were no instructions as to how to get home. This was something to be suspicious of. Her father always suspected other nations ran networks of spies in Galnesh Eldador.

When Hectaro was gone, she searched all of the saddle blankets, but she found nothing. This had happened too fast for another note. She called for her own saddle, letting her being travel outside of her body again, this time ready for the saddle to come flying out of the east. This time she caught her own light riding saddle, and she knew it had a note on it before she was back in her own body.

"I can help you," the note said. "Most people think you're dead. I knew better. Let me know where you are, and I'll come get you. –G– "

Her suspicion rose to the overt offer. A Princess has a lot of people looking to curry favor, and being able to do an actual favor made currying a lot easier. This would be an amazing accomplishment for someone trying to get on the inside.

It could even be Angron Aurelias himself, trying to get her back.

These notes hadn't actually done her any good. She owed this person nothing. She also had no idea how to communicate back with whoever was writing the notes.

She was getting stronger, that much she was sure of. Maybe she was building up the strength it would take to get a message back to her parents.

She started stacking the blankets. If they could keep some of them, they'd make good bedding. Who knew?

D'leer rose after the sun set. She noted the saddle and all of the blankets, regarding Lee with a raised eyebrow. Lee pushed past her into the hole in the hill and laid herself down to sleep. She'd had a big day and she was worn out.

She slept well into the next day. When she finally woke the two Wolf Soldiers were smoking meat from a gazelle and there were two horns, each three feet long, laying to one side with a hide stretched out in the sun. Singer had her saddle on her, meaning D'leer had been riding.

"We'll be ready to leave tonight?" she asked the two of them.

D'leer nodded. "Yes, Lee," she said, addressing her like she would her father. "The saddles are going to help a lot. We'll bundle up some of the blankets and bury the rest."

Lee nodded. She could see the meat needed a few more hours. There were a few steaks cut and cooked already, to one side.

"The two of you rest," she said. "I'll finish the meat. Unsaddle and put those horses up first."

"Yes, Lee," Hectaro said. They both went and do as they were told.

This is what she'd told herself she wanted from them. She was telling them what to do, they were doing it. Probably her magic had them scared. Maybe they were starting to think they were going to survive this. Who knew?

It wasn't as satisfying as she'd thought it would be, that much she knew. She'd wanted a friend in Hectaro and she'd ended up with a vassal.

Vassals didn't give a lot back, and she was starting to feel very lonely. In the back of her mind, she was afraid she was getting a look at her future life.

Her father didn't smile a lot, and maybe now she knew why.

48

Chapter Nine

In the Dark

The sun went down, the Wolf Soldiers rose. Lee had already made a role of five of the blankets and tied it up with two strips of leather, then wrapped up their two skins along with the horns and long bones from the gazelle. The rest she'd buried.

She'd made a rough kirruk with bones and skin, which she used to carry their remaining cloths. Their water bladders were tied with strips of woven leather over the pommels of their saddles. The horses were ready to go.

Hectaro raised his eyebrows and frowned appreciatively. D'leer didn't register anything. Both walked from the hollow to Bastard, saying nothing. Hectaro mounted the stallion and pulled the Uman woman up after him.

Lee tied up the rolled blankets behind her saddle, shrugged into the kirruk and mounted Singer. Together they walked out from behind the hill and toward the city.

"There's no trail," D'leer said. "You have to –"

"I know the way," Lee informed her, not looking at the two of them.

"You do?" D'leer pursued her.

When Lee didn't respond immediately, Hectaro said, "She's teaching herself to move her mind out over the land when she pulls these things back from Galnesh Eldador," he said. "She's getting really good at it."

D'leer turned her head to Lee, then back to Hectaro, then back and forth again. "You're practicing your magic on your own, then?" she asked.

Again, Lee didn't respond.

D'leer sighed. "The race of Men," she said.

"What's that supposed to mean," Lee asked.

The horses picked up a trot. The open plain called to them. Bastard loved to run and Singer was used to moving with him. She couldn't match his speed but she loved to open up, and she'd proved herself sure-footed.

D'leer adjusted on Bastard's flank. Bareback was hard on a trotting horse, the ride was rougher and she'd keep crashing into the back of Hectaro's saddle. Lee had experienced this on those rare occasions when she'd done the same on her father's horse.

"An Uman with your gifts would be twenty before she even thought to plumb them," she said. "Closer to thirty. An Uman-Chi would wait a century."

Hectaro smiled. "They're not as gifted as we are," he said.

Lee smiled.

D'leer didn't. "The Uman-Chi are the premier wizards on Fovea," she said.

Lee actually barked a laugh. "Tell that to my mother," she said. "Did they ever actually *find* the gates to Outpost IX."

When Lee had been just an infant when the Uman-Chi had worked with Volkhydran, Sentalan and Dorkan assassins to kill the then-queen of Eldador, when Lee's father had been just a Duke. The King of Eldador at the time, Glennen, had charged her father with his vengeance.

Her father had invaded Outpost IX, the capitol of Trenbon, home of the Uman-Chi and the kingdom of Angron Aurelias. Shela Mordetur had famously used her magic to blow the gates off of the city and launch them into Tren Bay.

A city of Wizards, and the Mordeturs had beaten them all. The act had shamed the nation – no one else had ever come close to such a victory over the long-lived Uman-Chi.

Lee was paying for her hubris now.

"Granted," D'leer said.

"But you're going too fast," she added. "Even your mother, gifted as she is, wasn't exercising this sort of power at so young an age. We're months' march from Galnesh Eldador, with a mountain range between. I don't think your mother could do what you're doing even now."

"Really?" Lee asked, then checked herself.

Both Wolf Soldiers smiled but neither commented.

Lee sighed. She put her heels to Singer's ribs and the horse picked up a canter. Bastard followed eagerly.

This was dangerous. A walking horse was exposed for longer, but the sun set to the west and it was pretty much down – the north where they crossed past the city was darkened and there was little to see.

A cantering stallion of Bastard's size, with his huge hooves, was plenty to hear. A city of farmers wouldn't be conducting loud parties all night – they could hear night sounds. Sound echoed strangely against a city's walls.

Singer tossed her head. She'd go faster if Lee let her; not a good idea in the dark. Also, if they did draw attention, they might need more speed later rather than now.

They pounded through the night. Lee remembered the way to the path from her out of body experience. She used her magic to enhance her own vision, gathering more light for her eyes. She immediately started picking out details and landmarks.

"Line Bastard up behind me," she shouted over her shoulder. Hectaro immediately reined the huge stallion over. Shouting was more dangerous than cantering and both knew it.

Toward the city, a tiny flame winked to life between them and the wall. It could be a shepherd tending a flock, a guard, anything. Regardless, they'd been heard.

As close as it was, they'd have been heard as easily at a trot, but not passed so quickly. People questioned what they couldn't see, but had a hard time when watching it passing.

She held her pace, looking out for fencing she might not have seen passing over. If there were flocks, there would be fencing.

Sure enough she caught glistening wire and pulled the reins to the left just before Singer would have been tangled. Bastard followed close behind as they drew away from the city. She'd follow the fencing until they could turn back to the mountains.

"Ow! War's beard!" she heard Hectaro swear. D'leer shushed him.

She wanted to look over her shoulder and see if that light was moving, but she didn't dare take her eyes off of their path. The logical decision was to stop but then if they were being followed...

Stupid she admonished herself. These people didn't ride.

She held up her hand, did an eight count and reined her horse in, giving Hectaro time to stop Bastard.

Hectaro, however, couldn't *see* her raised hand. He crashed right into Singer's rump. Singer neighed, Bastard reared and called out his challenge. D'leer flew off of the horse's rump and into the fence.

Singer kicked out twice and then settled. Hectaro got his mount under control, turning the stallion in a circle as Lee pulled her own horse back and gave the other space.

D'leer was groaning – the fence line was probably barbed, and she was doing what she could not to cry out in pain.

Lee looked to the south. There were three flames now where there had been one, and they were bouncing. People holding lanterns, coming to investigate. They might have passed them off as gazelle, but those didn't do a lot of swearing.

"Lee!" Hectaro hissed. "What's going on?"

"Shut up, Hectaro," she ordered him. "Stay mounted."

She leapt from Singer's back and passed Hectaro up her reins, touching them to his hand. She realized he was calling into the dark and she was likely nothing more than a dark blob in a dark setting to him.

She ran to D'leer's side, where the Uman woman was, indeed, caught in barbed wire.

"D'leer," she said.

"It's bad," she answered. She didn't need to say more. Whoever had strung the fence had gone five strands, meaning there were five lines of wire. D'leer had fallen half way through it, and her clothes were well tangled. It would take long minutes to cut her free.

D'leer pulled her dagger and handed it hilt-first to Lee.

"Make it quick," she said. "I don't want to be the first Wolf Soldier ever captured by the Confluni. We aren't friends."

And her father had rather famously tortured captured prisoners, Lee thought.

But there was a better way.

Beginning sorceresses learned what was known as 'utility magic,' useful spells to make life easier, just as they learned to heal before they learned to fight. One of the most common spells was to make a dull knife sharp. Another was to harden metal, which was useful when a tent stake was bent and needed to be straightened, to keep it from bending again.

"Hectaro," she called the young prince.

He dismounted. Lee unfocused her eyes and focused her will. She hardened the steel in the dagger, and she made the edge ultra sharp.

Hectaro reached out for her and she felt his hand on her shoulder. Past him, those flames were bobbing still.

She pressed the dagger into his hand. "Strike the wire," she said.

"The – what?" she could understand how she made no sense.

"Just do it," she ordered him.

She saw him shrug. "As hard as you can," she added. "If you're strong, it will break."

She knew the challenge would inspire him.

She focused on the wire, and she made it cold. Ice had a million uses.

Hectaro struck, the wire shattered. He struck again and again, and he hacked all five strands.

"The other side," she ordered him, and she took hold of D'leer.

The wire had to be tight for this to work.

Hectaro felt his way to her other side. Lee moved her hands to D'leer's body, felt her tunic, her shoulders, her over-large breasts. She felt D'leer reaching for her but the wire still restrained her.

Lee took a firm hold of D'leer. She focused her will and froze the wire on the other side.

She pulled hard on the Wolf Soldier uniform, hearing it start to tear. D'leer whimpered as the barbed wire bit her.

"Strike!" she commanded.

In a few strokes Hectaro was through four of the strands. On the last one the dagger shattered. The wire didn't break.

"Curse me!" Hectaro swore.

"I – I think I can do another dagger," she said, but she couldn't be sure. This was a lot of rapid-fire magic.

"No, wait," Hectaro answered her. She saw him feeling for the wire, find it, take it in both hands.

"It's cold," he commented.

He took the wire in both hands, near the barbs, and he started bending it back and forth, first slowly and then faster, wearing out the metal, breaking the bonds in the wire.

Lee took D'leer's other dagger from her belt, and she started cutting away her uniform.

It didn't take long. A good Wolf Soldier kept her weapons sharp, and D'leer had been an excellent Wolf Soldier.

She had the Uman woman naked except for a breech cloth in short time. To the south she could make out the forms of Confluni carrying lanterns. There were six. They were as close as a few minutes' run now, but of course, they couldn't see Lee, the horses and the Wolf Soldiers.

"We can't leave this uniform here," D'leer hissed.

"What?" Lee said. This was stupid – the uniform was ruined.

"It's a *Wolf Soldier* uniform," D'leer insisted. "If they find it, they'll think they're being invaded and they'll set up the alarm. Right now we're thieves."

And there was a big difference between thieves and invaders, Lee thought. D'leer was right.

The wire on the other side snapped. Hectaro stood. D'leer emerged topless from her uniform.

"Into the pasture," Hectaro said.

Both women hesitated.

"We roust the flock," he said. "The flock is their livelihood. No matter how they feel about us, they'll collect them first."

Lee nodded. "Remount," she said.

"The uniform," D'leer said.

"I have it," Lee said. "We cross the pasture. I can see in the dark, you have to follow. We don't want to get caught in the wire at the other side – stay behind me and to the north. When I see wire, I'll call out."

Both Wolf Soldiers nodded. They all mounted.

Lee had two wires on her right hand. The barbs had cut her and they hurt. She walked Singer through the hole in the fence and Bastard followed her.

Aurochs. She saw them now. They'd sensed the activity and they were sniffing near the fence. An aurochs was unpredictable and territorial – if they sensed the horses were coming into the pasture, they'd try to run them out.

Even better.

"Change of plans," she said. "Aurochs. Trot north. D'leer, go ahead and keep him from running into the fence."

"*Lee!*" Hectaro hissed.

She didn't have the time. She put her heels to her horse, skirting the herd to the left.

The aurochs were already starting to trot on their own, sensing an invader.

She focused her will again, and she made the Wolf Soldier uniform burst into flame.

Singer nickered to be so close to the fire. She took off at a canter and the wind fanned the flame. The flame brought the desired reaction from the aurochs. Some gave chase to her, some stampeded for the hole in the fence.

The Confluni with the lanterns started shouting. She could barely see D'leer and Bastard moving north. Lee made a circle around the pasture and got all of the aurochs running, then she made a beeline for the fence.

At first she couldn't find the hole they'd cut, then she saw it was clogged with aurochs. The Confluni were trying to use their torches to drive the aurochs back into the pasture. Lee wasn't going to get out that way.

The uniform was almost burned out. She dropped the wire and she ran for the north, her magic starting to wane. She'd done a lot tonight and she didn't have much left.

She found Bastard and the two Wolf Soldiers. She started trotting next to them. D'leer mounted up behind Hectaro, all but naked, and wrapped her arms around his waist. There was shouting, snorting and aurochs bellowing, all at the opening in the fence. Now that some were out, they were all pushing, some breaking for the fence or getting caught up in it.

It didn't take long for them to come to the northeast corner of the fence, a wooden triangle reinforced with stones at its base.

Hectaro turned Bastard's butt to it and reined him in, then whipped his flank with the reins. D'leer hissed in pain.

Bastard kicked out and connected with the wooden post. The post cracked.

Hectaro dismounted and pushed the post over. Lee dismounted as well and walked singer over the fallen fence.

They had time now. There were other things on the Confluni's mind

Chapter Ten

Mountain Girl

They followed the fence to the other side of the city, and from there they found their way past another field, another set of shepherds, and to a trail leading to the mountain pass. From there they picked their way in the dark, Lee and Hectaro leading the horses up a torturous trail.

Hectaro had given his tunic to D'leer, and she'd managed to retain her boots. She was scratched in dozens of places, most of them quite deep, and Lee didn't have the strength to heal her *and* give herself the night vision she needed to guide them.

The wounds would begin to heal on their own. When that happened it left a sorceress little to add. Much as an old wound can't be stitched, the magic that would heal it finds no target to work with.

This left D'leer open to infection and scarring. A Wolf Soldier always carried a vial of alcohol and a pouch of witch hazel, but D'leer had lost hers and Hectaro wasn't sure he had enough. The aurochs notoriously rubbed on the barbed wire and rolled in their own feces in the pasture. The chance of an infection setting in was good.

But it wouldn't help D'leer if they walked off of a cliff or waited for the light and were captured by the Confluni, either.

Behind them, they saw Confluni lanterns by the dozen, bobbing through the night. The aurochs would likely find their way to the crops before enough shepherds could arrive to stop them. Some would undoubtedly be lost, along with portions of their crop both eaten and trampled. This would represent a huge loss to the city, and make for some angry farmers.

Angry farmers usually got it into their heads that someone needed to pay.

Considering this, Lee and the Wolf Soldiers marched into the night. The path wound back and forth up the side of the mountain, providing a gradual slope rather than one steep trail which would be treacherous to climb in rainy weather or even harder to descend at any time. They reached a plateau of sorts after climbing for more than an hour and the trail started to wind around the mountain rather than to climb it. In two more hours this put the mountain between them and the city.

"Oh, I can't *believe* it!" Lee exclaimed, as they passed out of site of the city.

"What?" Hectaro asked her. The temperature had dropped at least ten degrees and he was shivering a little without his tunic. D'leer couldn't have felt much better.

"We didn't drag our tracks," Lee said.

An Andaron raider trick; one dragged a skin or brush behind the horses and obscured the tracks they left. At the very least they went single-file to confuse their numbers. Lee had done neither. The Confluni would see the horse tracks leading right into the mountains, right from the chaos they had caused.

A xenophobic race, the Confluni tolerated no outsiders in their nation. They'd go to any ends to track them down. As far as anyone knew, they didn't ride.

"I could go back…" Hectaro began.

"No," Lee told him. "You wouldn't be able to see the tracks, and you couldn't stay on the trail. If I go, you're stuck here and I wouldn't be back before the dawn. That's if we haven't been discovered already.

"Bastard is a distinctive horse," she added. "They're going to see those tracks and they're going to know someone riding a *very* large horse came through here, and who knows what they'll think?"

Lee's father rode a stallion named, "Blizzard." Bastard was only slightly smaller, being sired by that horse.

How could she be so stupid! she berated herself. She had the skin on a roll behind her horse.

"Nothing to be done f-f-f-f-for it," D'leer spoke up, her teeth chattering. "We can walk 'till the sun comes up, then we'll ride as fast as we can. They have no horses so they'll know we're outsiders, but they won't be able to c-c-c-c-c-catch us."

They did just that, moving silently, the only sound the snorting from the horses. Different things went through Lee's mind. Was there a spell or incantation she could use to cover or re-route their tracks? Did the Confluni use birds to communicate between cities? Could they start an avalanche and block the trail from behind?

That last sounded good, and her father had done something similar before she was born to win a battle with the Dwarves against the Dorkan people, but she didn't know much about their craft and she would as likely bring the mountain down on herself.

Her energy was depleted and this walking was telling on her. She called two stops during the night to eat and to water the horses. She could have eaten all of their supplies if she'd been less careful, and a few strips of jerked meat left her barely less hungry than before.

She needed to replenish her energy or it would take *forever* to be able to cast again.

Finally the sun rose up over the mountains, first the red false dawn, then the true light of the actual sun rise. Lee welcomed the lightning of the cloudy sky above and before them.

Her attention went first to D'leer – the Uman had done worse in the barbed than she'd let on. Black trails of dried blood ran down her body and into the horse's fur beneath her. Deep gouges ran down her arms and across her abdomen, even dotting her breasts in places. One scar ran down her back from her scapula to her waist.

Hectaro hissed as he saw it, peeling off her tunic. D'leer sat quiet as they took one of Lee's cloths from her dress, wetted it and washed her. Lee had seen this behavior before in warriors who'd suffered grievous wounds – they detached their minds from their bodies and didn't wince from the pain because it was too much for their bodies to register.

She'd learned these were the warriors you lost.

Hectaro searched her eyes, saying nothing.

If she ate all of their supplies and then slept for a day, she'd probably be able to save D'leer, but then it would be pointless. She could do a little now but even a little effort would weaken her dangerously.

She couldn't afford to have that conversation with them, either. If they lost faith in her, they'd lose faith in the mission, and they would fail.

"It's too late to stitch these," she informed them, standing over D'leer where she sat on the ground, Hectaro squatting next to her. "And that means it's too late to heal her with magic."

"Are you sure about that?" Hectaro questioned her. As the son of a Duke, he'd been educated in what he could ask for from a wizard.

But not necessarily a sorceress.

"What I do works with the body," she said, not the whole truth but not a lie, either. "The body is already doing what it's doing.

"Clean her well. I have an underskirt left she can wear. We'll keep her as warm as we can and we'll push as fast as we dare. There's a river on the other side of these mountains and the clean running water will do more for her than I can."

Hectaro nodded and D'leer stared at the ground. The horses cropped at scrub growing along the path. There was enough grass and small plants here to tell Lee this trail hadn't been used in a while. It was probably for moving the harvest, meaning there wasn't a caravan likely to meet them half way to their destination.

Their tracks were plain as day behind them. When she found a likely place for an accident, she'd walk the horses to the edge, fake a couple more tracks and then cause a small landslide, then start dragging their skin behind them. It might make any pursuers think they'd gone over a cliff in the dark, and at the least hold them up investigating.

"To the sky!" Hectaro cried out, pointing to the west.

All three turned to see a flock of birds winging their way east. No doubt what this was – small birds moving fast meant messengers.

Lee felt weak, but she'd feel weaker if she had to fight her way out of the mountains through a waiting army. She raised her hand, white with power, and she unfocused her eyes.

There were incantations which were used to make animals sleep so they could be slaughtered. She used such an incantation now, focusing on the birds.

The birds were actually more than a daheer above her, which made for a long way, and there were several of them, spread out over dozens of cubic yards. A bird had a simple mind, but there were ten of them.

Her knees buckled as they fell out of the sky. Hectaro ran to her side, she took the spare material from his trousers in her left hand to steady herself, and felt his hand on her shoulder.

She scanned the sky, her vision wavering in and out. She searched for more birds but she couldn't be sure.

The sky grew dark as she lost consciousness.

Chapter Eleven

Over the Hump

Lee awoke bouncing, the strong smell of a horse's sweat in her nose, its fur in her face. It took a moment to realize she'd been tied over the back of her mare.

Her wrists and ankles were bound. Despite herself, she started screaming.

"No, no, Lee, no, it's alright, it's alright," she heard, then felt Hectaro's hand on the small of her back. She tried to look up but her stiff neck resisted her. She felt fingers on the leather thongs on her wrists, and then she was free and starting to slide off of the horse's back.

Hectaro tried to catch her as she fell helpless to the rocky ground. Singer pranced forward and then stopped, turning to regard her. Lee rolled over onto her back, feeling the dust in her hair, and saw D'leer sitting Bastard's back, staring vacantly in her direction.

Hectaro untied the long leather strip from her ankles. She realized what had happened – she'd lost consciousness and they'd tied her over her horse's back so they could keep moving. She'd have done the same thing.

She tried to rise but couldn't. Hectaro fetched her water and a hand full of jerked meat.

"Eat," he told her.

"That's too much," she said.

He shook his head. "We'll find more, or we'll do without, or you'll call it from Galnesh Eldador. A wizard needs to eat, a sorceress is no different. You're worn out and weak and you need your strength."

She wanted to argue but she couldn't. Once she bit down on the first strip of dried meat she almost went into a feeding frenzy, and ate more than she planned to allow herself in three days.

She had an idea of how wide this mountain range was. She didn't think they'd have enough to get them across now.

Finally she stood, feeling a *lot* better. She looked to the sky, expecting to see flocks of birds.

Hectaro followed her gaze and nodded. "I've been watching," he said. "I haven't seen anything – a few hawks, that's it. No one uses a hawk as a messenger bird."

She nodded. In fact, you could use a hawk, but she didn't want to argue with him.

There was no point.

D'leer didn't speak the entire time. Lee had Hectaro help her down and she inspected the woman, finding what she expected.

D'leer was already burning up with fever. The ride was doing her no good. She gave the Uman water and then felt the weight of the bladder, finding it surprisingly full.

"There are water caches every few daheeri," he said. "We've been drinking as much as we can and keeping our skins full. The grain we packed for the horses is holding out and they've found some graze. I think we might come out hungry but we'll make it."

Lee's eyes moved between Hectaro and D'leer until he caught the significance. They might not *all* make it.

There was nothing for it.

"How far have we come?" Lee asked.

Hectaro shrugged. "Hard to tell in the mountains," he said. "You might go all day and only cross a daheer. We've kept a respectable pace and we haven't come across anything more than a rockslide to slow us, so the best I can say is we're going as fast as we can, or at least as fast as we should."

That got a little smile from her. Hectaro's charm couldn't be denied. She rubbed her wrists and ankles where the leather thongs had chaffed her and she stepped up to her horse. She took a fist full of mane and pulled herself up into the saddle.

Singer stepped back a little but kept steady. Lee frowned. The mare might be getting too much water but she didn't think so. The sweat on her withers looked about right.

She gave the horse her heels and she took off at a trot. Out of habit she felt for a limp or a hesitation but there was nothing. Singer was moving as she always moved. Still, a rider knows her horse and Lee rode no less than four times a week. Something wasn't right with the mare and she needed to identify it.

They came across another water cache a little more than an hour later and they stopped to let the horses drink and to fill the bladder Lee had partially emptied. She made D'leer drink and relieve herself, and then she made Hectaro lead Singer back and forward, noting nothing. She checked the mare's hooves and found them sound, then she patted Singer on the rump out of habit.

The horse kicked out at her, barely missing her shoulder. Lee leapt out of the way and went for the bridle, catching the horse before she could bolt. This wasn't like Singer *at all.*

"I was afraid of that," Hectaro said.

"What?" Lee felt frustrated. She counted herself an excellent horsewoman and didn't want to think Hectaro would catch anything she might miss.

"That horse is about to go into season," he said. "She's been testy all day and she's been wanting to crowd Bastard. You've never bred her, have you?"

Lee shook her head, stepping back up to Singer's side and taking her chestnut mane in her hand. She rubbed the powerful neck muscles until the mare pitched her ears forward, then she positioned herself to mount again.

Warriors had been handling mares in estrus around stallions since the first mounted campaign, and she knew what it took to keep a regular stallion complacent. This was *not*, however, a regular stallion, this was a first-generation son of a horse from the Herd That Cannot be Tamed, and almost every horse her father's horse, Blizzard, had sired had been too wild or too unpredictable to ride. Most believed Bastard, out of an Andaron mare, had Hectaro to thank for being ridable at all. Hectaro had spent almost every day working with the stallion, from its birth to this moment.

The scent of a mare in heat might be more than Hectaro could control. Stallions killed their riders, trampled fences and performed a score of other irrational acts when they smelled mares in that condition.

She mounted and once again Singer backed up. If she'd had a crop she'd have disciplined the animal right then, as it was she pounded her ribs with her heels and made her move forward.

Singer took off at a trot with Bastard right after her. Even this wasn't a safe condition to ride. The stallion should be kept ahead of the mare in estrus.

"Hectaro, pass me," Lee ordered him. She reined the mare in and to one side.

Singer was having none of it. Without warning she took off, pushing off with both back feet. Bastard immediately took up chase, doing exactly what the mare wanted from him. She wanted to run and be chased. She'd found herself a good stallion and she was ready to be bred.

The fact it was on a mountain trail barely wider than an ox cart didn't matter a bit to either of them.

Lee pulled back on the reins with all of the strength in her but Singer ignored her. Whether she'd gotten the bit into her teeth or she'd just decided to take the pain was impossible to tell right then. The Andaron mare ran the mountain pass like she would have done the broad, Andoron plains, her legs stretching out and her back-and-forward gate more a gallop than a canter. They came up on a turn in the pass and Singer took it on her front hooves, barely slowing. Bastard, larger and more top heavy, had his back feet slide out from him and barely recovered before he pitched himself and his riders into an abyss more than a daheer deep. From there it was a straight climb up the side of a mountain at an incline that must have been terrifying to the wagoneers who used this pass, and Singer addressed it pushing out with both back feet, leaving a dust cloud behind her which left Hectaro and D'leer both choking.

Normally Lee would take a runaway like this into a circle and keep it turning until it finally realized it wasn't getting anywhere. There was no room for such a maneuver, and Singer had been trained by Andarons, in fact by her own uncle as a gift to her. If Lee ran her into the mountain side to stop her she'd happily crash her body into it, and then likely injure herself and probably take the skin off of Lee's leg in the process. If Singer wanted to ignore the bit, Lee was going to go along for the ride.

They climbed the steep rise, topped it and found a decline only a little less steep on the other side. Singer called out and took the decline at a canter, Bastard still behind her. Lee could see a somewhat sharp turn at the bottom and couldn't tell what might be on the other side of it.

Too fast, she knew. It was easily two daheeri to the turn, and Singer was picking up speed. She'd never make the turn at the end – she'd roll and kill them both or just leap into the open air instead. She had to start slowing the mare *now*, and she'd have to hope Hectaro did the same and the larger Bastard didn't crash into the back of them and knock them over the side anyway.

She pulled back on the bit and pitched her feet forward in the stirrups for leverage. Singer snorted and ducked her chin; Lee took a shorter grip on the reins and actually tucked the horse's chin against its neck.

Singer dropped her butt and went into a slide, pitching gravel and dust all around her. Now Bastard would have a hard time seeing her, if he even stopped at all. There were horses trained to slide like this, but such training went more for cattle horses and required special shoes. Singer was likely doing herself real harm right now, and Lee couldn't think of a thing she could do to stop it.

The mare came to a stop half a daheer from the bottom. Singer shook her head and collected herself to rise when Lee heard, "War's whiskers" from behind her and felt more than saw the tremendous weight of a 17 hand stallion bearing down on her from behind.

Bastard sailed over them, a rear hoof catching Lee's shoulder painfully and then grazing Singer's neck. Bastard landed on the other side of the both of them, then tried to lope to a stop, bouncing and neighing, finally rearing to stop his forward motion.

D'leer sailed off of his rump and hit the ground, bouncing and then rolling behind them. Bastard crashed into the mountain side, bounced off of it and finally stopped with a few yards to spare from the bottom. He collected himself, turned and Lee could see the bloody rags which was the left leg of Hectaro's pants.

They'd survived this, but at what cost?

Chapter Twelve

Where Bad Meets Worse

Lee felt pretty sure she hadn't broken her shoulder, but it definitely *felt* like she had. The bruise would have had her little brother begging her to see it hourly.

Hectaro had enough grit and cloth ground into the bloody skin on his leg to fill a small bag, and Lee almost lost her meal twice trying to wash it out.

D'leer lay unconscious when they found her and three hours later, as the sun set, her condition hadn't changed. They'd made a camp at the turn in the road, where they realized they'd have sailed off a cliff into oblivion if they hadn't managed to stop the horses.

The horses had suffered multiple abrasions from the run. Singer had taken the fur from her hide and worn herself a red patch on her flank from her stop. Bastard's blood had mixed with his rider's on the mountain side, his left whither deeply scratch from the stony wall.

Lee's magic let her heal them enough to bear riders, but it left her depleted once again. There was nothing for it- the horses bore them, they needed to be sound. The three of them could be injured and still ride.

While Lee was wrapping Hectaro's leg, hoping they had enough witch hazel left to keep the infection out, Bastard mounted Singer and there was no stopping him. A horse could be ridden for months after being seeded – this wouldn't be a problem for them to address this year.

But Bastard was more than a hand taller than Singer, and she might easily bear a foal big enough to kill her. Lee really loved Singer and didn't want to see her die that way.

"Your mother might have some magic..." Hectaro said.

"If we find her in time," Lee snapped at him. "If we aren't caught by the Confluni, if she's not still on campaign when we're back to Galnesh Eldador. There's nothing we can do for it now, Hectaro, and I can't worry about it. We'll deal with whatever happens when it happens."

Lee blamed herself for the situation they were in. She knew her horse was in estrus, she knew what estrus meant and she'd tried to act like she could ignore it. Yes, the stallion should have led the two of them, but a mare in heat was an unpredictable thing and, as soon as Bastard had approached her, she'd acted just as a mare in her condition might be expected to act. How many times had her mother told her, "The horse you love the most will be the one who hurts you worst."? In the end they are animals, and animals do what they do and don't understand if you love them and want what's best for them.

They didn't have a fire because they didn't have any wood. They went to feed and realized one of Bastard's bags had shattered against the mountain side. They'd lost a fourth of their grain into the dust. Lee could go back and try to collect it when the sun came up, but she expected to find a swarm of whatever small animals lived in the mountains to beat her to it.

It would be a miracle if they made it through the mountains in the state they were in.

They laid down to sleep under a night sky without a moon or stars, which seemed very strange to Lee, but she didn't remark on it to Hectaro because she didn't want to talk to him. She closed her eyes and imagined herself telling the story of their wild ride to her brother and her parents, her little sister in her lap.

Her brother had left to campaign with their father and probably had much wilder tales to tell. Her mother would likely admonish her and come up with some patently obvious solution Lee had never thought of to end the ride. Her father would commend 'his brave girl' but he wouldn't mean it.

She'd welcome it all, she thought, as sleep took her.

***

She awoke to D'leer moaning. Every fiber of her being told her to roll over and ignore it but the sorceress in her was a servant to the sick, and D'leer, traitor that she was, was still her responsibility.

She pushed herself up from the horse blanket she slept on and her body all but screamed in protest. Every muscle punished her for her wild ride and her shoulder felt like it would leap from her body, turn around and slap her.

The first rain drops struck her face right then.

"Oh, by Law," she swore. Of course. No stars, no moon. The storm had rolled in after the sun went down and now it was going to rain.

In the mountains, with them at the bottom of a steep, straight trail.

Well, she thought. *Why not? Why should it be easy for her? A Princess' life should be a trial, after all.*

"Oh, gods, it's raining," Hectaro informed her unnecessarily.

"Tend D'leer," she ordered him. "We have to get away from here. I'll collect the horses and try to save our supplies."

"What?" Hectaro stood. Of course he wanted to argue. Of course he'd pick right now to defy her.

"We're at the bottom of a wash, Hectaro," she snarled at him. "As soon as the real rain starts, we're going to be battling for our footing and everything touching the ground, ourselves included, is going over that cliff. Would you like to experience that?"

"Oh," he said. She detected the sullenness in his voice. She didn't have time to rescue his male ego.

"We have to ride for high ground," she said. "Do what I told you."

She used her magic to enhance her sight again and found the horses where they'd been hobbled, side-by-side against the mountain. Bastard was shielding the smaller mare from the weather.

She knew what *that* meant. It was going to be bad.

She found their horse blankets, picked a dry one and spread it on Bastard's back, getting all of the wrinkles out by habit. Then she heaved Hectaro's military saddle onto the stallion's back and cinched it as tight as she could. She fitted the heavy bridle and then pulled

Bastard away from Singer so she could do the same with her own horse.

The rain was becoming a drizzle. D'leer was moaning.

"She feels like she's on fire," Hectaro commented.

"The rain will cool her," Lee said. Hopefully she was right. She couldn't be sure, but she needed to address the issue and she needed to get Hectaro's mind right. "Your horse is ready. Follow my voice and get her over his back."

"She can't ride," Hectaro argued.

Lee sighed. "Tie her like a gazelle if you have to," she ordered him. "We have to go, that's it."

She could see Hectaro stand with D'leer in his arms. The Uman lay limp with her head against his shoulder, her nearly-naked body glistening with a mixture of rain and sweat. For a moment Lee thought it might be a mercy to just chuck her over the mountainside and immediately admonished herself for the thought. It sounded like something her father would say.

Maybe she was starting to understand why he seemed so mean all the time.

She got her blanket and saddle and readied her own horse. Singer was a different animal now and actually rubbed her nose on her upper arm and budding breasts. Lee buckled her own saddle into place and fit the bit to Singer's mouth. She found the rest of the blankets, their leather supply and their water bladders, stowing them in the increasing rain.

A trickle was already starting down the mountain toward them. They didn't have long.

She pulled herself up into the saddle and pushed her horse forward. Hectaro and D'leer followed, the Uman moaning from where Hectaro had slung her like a bed roll behind his saddle. Around the corner, the trail was again barely more than an ox-cart wide, to their right the rough, hand-carved mountain wall, to their left empty space filled with increasing rain.

Even her enhanced sight had trouble in the increasing rain. She started needing to use more power to divert a little of the rain from her head, and felt herself begin to weaken. An hour into the storm the path held narrow and flat against the mountain and the wind and rain lashed them mercilessly. The horses snorted and D'leer whimpered, and for a little extra incentive Hectaro complained once in a while that they might be safer if they just stayed put.

Lee knew better. Lightning might start at any moment, and the horses would react to it. If they were on horseback when lightning hit the ground then anything could happen. They needed to find a wide space which wasn't at the bottom of a hill, where they could be protected or at least dismounted.

She was just starting to wonder who would build a trail like this and expect caravans to travel for days through the mountains with no protection from the elements, when the mountainside opened up to their right. She sensed more than felt a wide, open cavern to her right, and she used her enhanced sight to explore it.

Nothing. She half expected a mountain cat or something equally nasty to take a swipe at her and strip her from her saddle, but nothing. The cavern was deeper than she could see into it and taller than Hectaro on his horse's back. She pushed her mount into the open space, the mare shivering and uncertain beneath her, and Bastard followed. They both sat quiet, listening, waiting, but they heard nothing. This had been carved here to give a caravan exactly what the three of them needed: protection from the elements.

"I think we're safe here," Lee said, finally. "This cavern is huge and I don't see anything in it. Why don't you dismount and get D'leer's clothes off, and we'll wrap her in the horse blankets."

From within the cavern, they heard, "Who said that?"

Chapter Thirteen

Travelers

Lee winced in pain as a torch sprung to life in the cavern, scoring her eyes with her enhanced vision. She heard Hectaro's sword leap from its sheath behind her, and the clatter of horses' hooves as he pulled Bastard to one side. He'd charge if he could – everything depended on the layout revealed by the torchlight.

She dropped the spell to enhance her vision and heard Hectaro chuckle.

"And wot is this, then?" she heard ahead of her.

As her sight cleared, she looked down from her horse's back and saw the tiny people whom she recognized as the Scitai – a diminutive people smaller than Dwarves, native to the Silent Isle where the Uman-Chi lived.

What were they doing in Conflu?

"We're travelers," Hectaro said when she didn't reply. "We've got a sick woman with us, if we can come in out of the weather?"

Lee counted twelve of them, dressed in the browns and tans Scitai loved. Five were males and of them two had beards. The rest were females, two of them very old and the rest of varying ages. Scitai lived as long as Uman, about twice as long as Men, and their age could be hard to tell as they could often be confused with children and sported apple cheeks and unblemished skin.

"You're travelers come a long way, is sure," one bearded Scitai noted. He was standing forward as a leader. He'd cut his hair short and wore a little gray in it, his brown eyes searching Hectaro's. His homespun shirt was all of one piece stitched under the arms and bunched around the neck, tan in color, and he wore shaggy wolf-skin pants and boots made of skins, the silver fur brushed out.

He had a sword barely more than a long dagger at his hip but he hadn't pulled it. The Scitai were all excellent archers but Lee didn't see their bows.

"Will you let us in?" Hectaro asked again.

The Scitai turned his back on the three of them and spoke in a hushed voice to the others. D'leer moaned behind Hectaro. One of the women separated herself and scurried over to D'leer's head, where she was tied over Bastard's back. She felt the Uman's skin and her face showed her shock.

"Korrock," she said, "this one won't live the night through."

They spoke more. The older women seemed adamantly against this. The males seemed to be trying to placate them, while the younger women, all of them including the one by D'leer dressed in white embroidered skirts and tan homespun blouses like Korrock's, kept arguing that this wasn't their problem.

Finally Korrock turned back around, one of the older women next to him. "I am Korrock of the One Mountain," he said, "and this is my mother, Pieren. If you'll shed your weapons, then you're welcome to spend the night, and my mother will tend your sick."

Hectaro nodded without a single look at Lee. She knew what he was doing. They'd assumed he was their leader and he would let them believe it. This made things safer for Lee, although more dangerous for him if they were up to no good.

He pulled his sheath from over his shoulder and dropped it on the ground next to his horse. He pulled both daggers from his belt, one from his boot, a steel rod from his left sleeve, and a paring knife from his right. *The paring knife*, Lee thought, *was probably for eating, but why provoke them?*

"We are unarmed," he said.

"And the women?" Pieren asked, pointing a stubby index finger at Lee.

"She doesn't fight," he said. "She's my cousin, I safeguard her passage."

"Dismount, dismount," the woman by D'leer said. "Get her down where we can treat her."

Hectaro swung a leg wide over D'leer and dismounted by her head. He untied the leather thong holding her wrists and slid her over Bastard's side, making sure she didn't move behind and get kicked.

The woman took D'leer's feet and guided her across the cavern to the rock wall, where a pile of furs lay by a stream running down the wall and into a hole in the floor.

"Here, here, set her down here," she said. "Pieren, she's got the fever – surprised she's living, she's so hot."

"Well, maybe she won't live, Tooken," Pieren said, and limped after the younger Scitai to their Uman patient. "But the girl's an Uman, and Uman are hearty. We'll do what can be done for her."

"Tooken and Pieren will see to the woman," Korrock said, approaching Lee. "And you've a fine bad guardian as would bring Eldadorians into the deep of Conflu. Are you separated from a caravan or the last of it?"

Caravan, Lee wondered, but then she realized he'd mistaken Bastard for a draft. Confluni didn't ride and of course Scitai wouldn't know horses. If this were what he wanted to believe of them, she decided on the spot she'd best play into it.

"Captured from our caravan," she said, loud enough for Hectaro to hear. Any leader worthy of the title would try to separate them and get their stories, finding out what matched and what didn't. "We're out of Andaron –" she began.

"Ooo – look at 'is leg!" Tooken was poking at Hectaro's blackened clothing where the blood on his leg had dried and matted cloth to skin. "Off! Off with these! No time to be modest! No Scitai woman wants your giant Man parts!"

Hectaro barely defended himself as Tooken and another woman pulled his pants off.

The other four males crowded around Korrock and Lee. Her father's good friend and Daff Kanaar ally, Karel of Stone, was a Scitai, and Lee knew him well. He'd taught her their language and how to shoot arrows from a small cross-pistol his people liked. He was a notorious lecher and it seemed his kinsmen here were no different.

"Well this one's barely away from her mother's teat," one said.

"Still, ripe enough for a cold night," another added.

"Enough of that," Korrock warned. "Be civil to a strange girl in a strange land – we won't have her up all night guarding her virginity. Fear not, girl – these men only talk sport."

"I'll trust to your hospitality, my Lords," Lee said, and meekly lowered her head. She looked to one side and could see Hectaro had already had his pants stripped off and cast aside and a Scitai woman was scrubbing his leg with a wet rag. It must have opened up again while riding, and Hectaro must have swallowed the pain.

Her own shoulder cried out to her but she ignored it. The males guided her to sit by a little fire they started under a cast iron hood hanging down from the ceiling, and pushed a cold broth into her hands. They gave her a wooden spoon and she ate of it gratefully.

Meat and carrots and a little potato – they had themselves a garden somewhere.

The Scitai of the Silent Isle were good friends of her father, but more because they hated their Uman-Chi overlords. Karel had frequently voiced his disdain for Men and Uman alike. These people might have decided to take them in from the storm, but Lee didn't allow herself to be lulled into false confidence.

This could turn against them the moment these good people could get a runner back to the city they'd left.

***

Lee didn't know when she drifted off, but she awoke with the sun shining in through the cavern mouth and her horses roped off to one side of the cavern with straw at their feet. Someone had stripped their saddles, blankets, bits and bridles off and stacked them neatly past their rope wall, on the inside of the cavern.

Hectaro lay next to her with an arm around her middle, dressed in a long night shirt. She was dressed similarly and had no memory of donning it.

D'leer lay by well in a pile of furs. Lee watched her for a moment, long enough to see her chest rise and fall. The Uman woman was still alive.

Korrock sat on a stool beside Hectaro with a pipe in his hand, regarding her. Three of the women, Tuppen and two of the younger ones, were poking at a cook fire and a black kettle sitting in it.

"Good morning to you, sweet girl," he said to her.

She sat up, pushing Hectaro aside. "And to you."

"You slept a good portion," he said. "We put bay root in the broth to ease your healing."

She knew bay root – it was a sedative her mother had taught her. If you took too much you'd crave it. She only used it on the very sick and the dying.

Also good for prisoners, she knew. Get them addicted and they'd do anything to get more.

Her shoulder felt a lot better – it *was* good for healing, regardless.

"You'll be staying a few days, I think," he said. It wasn't a question.

A few days for the runners they'd sent to the city they just left to get there and come back with a troop of warriors.

"What are Scitai doing in Conflu?" she asked.

Korrock grinned, took a long drag from his pipe, and then blew a smoke ring. "Some say we were here first," he said. "Conflu is the original land of the Cheyak, and when they passed, their Confluni slaves moved in. The Scitai served the Cheyak to the end of their days."

The Cheyak, Lee knew, were the original people of Fovea, beloved of the god Power, who had displeased him and been overthrown more than 1,100 years ago.

They were the ancestors of the Uman-Chi, who claimed to have both Uman and Cheyak roots. People argued sometimes that the Scitai were pets to the Cheyak.

Korrock didn't seem like anyone's pet.

"You serve the Confluni now, then?" she asked him.

Hectaro should have roused up but didn't. They'd identified him as a threat and probably doped him pretty well. D'leer wouldn't be a problem in her condition. Lee was just a young girl and no one to worry about.

She suppressed a smile.

"We work with them," Korrock said. "We recognized his Wolf Soldier uniform, though. We might have let a traveler find their way back to the Jeng-Jeng River and out to Andoron, but not a Wolf Soldier scouting party. We're well aware the Emperor invaded Eldador, so we're not surprised there are Wolf Soldiers scouting Conflu to return the favor."

These Scitai didn't know who she was. She'd met the Confluni Emperor years ago, however. There was a good chance he'd recognize her. In fact, regular Wolf Soldier prisoners were highly unlikely to make it back so far, but if D'leer recovered then Lee didn't doubt she'd use any leverage to get herself a better deal.

Or give it up under torture.

Lee turned her head. The cavern could have housed two hundred Men. In the light she could see food stuffs and baled hay, stacks of clothing and shelves with tools and stacked wooden planking. This was a way-station in the mountains the Scitai maintained, and the distance they'd crossed in a few days was probably a week's journey for a caravan. This wouldn't be the only one, she was sure, but at least now she knew to be on her guard.

She didn't see anyone else here. She could see where they'd stacked their weapons by their saddles and blankets, well away from her and right where it would be easy to hand over to the Confluni who came to pick them up.

A Scitai male would be hard pressed to handle Hectaro – in fact three wouldn't be enough if he weren't drugged. Three women and one man probably felt more confident, but there should be another male…

Another of them, a male with no beard, strolled in through the cavern mouth. Yes, that made more sense.

Her mother hadn't taught her offensive magic, but she'd instilled in her a need to be creative.

Lee unfocused her eyes. Korrock said something to her but she didn't catch it. She knew where Hectaro's sword was now – that's all she needed.

The sword flew out from its sheath and the pommel caught the other male Scitai in the forehead, flattening him. The weapon clattered to the floor, then rose and rocketed straight for the cook pot.

The Scitai women screamed, Korrock stood and threw his pipe aside, reaching for his thigh. Karel of Stone often kept a collapsible bow in the same place.

The sword clanged against the cook pot, dumping its steaming contents on two of the Scitai women. Lee clamped down on her will and directed its sharpened point at Korrock.

The Scitai pulled a bow from his thigh where it must have been concealed in a flap of his trousers. He looked up in surprised as the sword crossed the room and bore down on him like one of the arrows he probably meant for her.

He tried to leap out of the way and the side of the blade took him across the back of the shoulder. He dropped to the floor as Lee leapt up and grabbed the weapon out of the air.

Tuppen already had a bow in her hand. Lee whistled and the bowstring snapped. Andarons had been using this same spell against the Aschire for years.

The two Scitai women were screaming. The one man by the entrance lay still. Lee took the sword handle two-handed, one over the other, and pressed the point against Korrock's back.

"On his life," she said, speaking like a Mordetur now, "you'll turn around and put your hands against the cavern wall."

"I've got injured – " she began.

Lee pressed the blade point into Korrock's back, drawing blood. The Scitai male screamed.

Tuppen ran to the cave wall, the other women limping after her.

Right then it occurred to Lee, she had no idea what to do next.

Chapter Fourteen

On Again

She could have used her magic to contain these few Scitai, but the act would have drained her, and she didn't know if she'd need her power later.

She *should* have killed them. Her mother would have. You grew up hard on the Andoron plains, where tribes counted what they called 'coupe,' a way of measuring their own status through bold acts and accomplishments, like kidnapping and raping a rival's daughter, or stealing all of their cattle.

Shela wouldn't have hesitated to kill every one of these Scitai who'd tried to turn them over to the Confluni. In fact, she might have thought it was funny.

Lee's father, the Emperor, actually possessed a kinder heart. He might carve his way through an enemy army with the point of his sword, but he'd weep over the body of a trampled puppy, and he didn't like to kill, even if he seemed to be very good at it.

In this Lee favored her father. She didn't kid herself into thinking of the Scitai as children. The Scitai were both cunning and deadly with their arrows, and would kill as mercilessly with them as the Andarons. No – these were not children, but these were people trying to live as best they could, and they had no reason to help invaders, especially not invaders in the uniforms of the most feared warriors on the planet, in favor of their own countrymen.

In Lee's opinion, too many people died for the same reason, and she didn't want to contribute to it.

She lined them up against the far wall, and she searched them all. She found daggers, collapsible bows, cross pistols, arrows more like darts and even garroting wire on all of them. She threw it all into the fire, and she threw more sticks on top of these to stoke it.

They weren't tall enough to saddle the horses for her, and a little of her magic told her they weren't lying when they said they had no antidote for the bay root they'd pumped into Hectaro. She made them pull saddle bags for her and she made them pack them tight with provisions. She made them undress and took their own rope and tied them wrist-to-ankle on the floor, making a circle of them and pouring oil on their hands. Even if they could turn their wrists around and pull at the knots she'd tied, their fingers would betray them and the oil-soaked ropes would be nearly impossible to untie.

She didn't speak to them if she didn't have to. She knew better. They all tried to engage her and she said nothing because this was an escape, not a debate, and every unnecessary second endangered her.

She pulled Hectaro out of his bedding and she dressed him. He started to rise groggily and to respond to her. The bay root would fight him and leave him suggestible, but while he wouldn't be able to fight, he *would* be able to ride, which was good enough.

D'leer was another matter.

The woman was unconscious but it seemed her fever had broken. No amount of shaking could rouse her, and the magic it would take to restore her would have left Lee shaking and useless.

Here, every fiber of her being told Lee to cut this woman's throat. The princess couldn't lift the Uman Wolf Soldier onto Bastard's back and Lee didn't have the time to engineer something to leverage her so high. Floating a sword around the cavern had been a little drain, raising the body of a full-grown Uman woman a man's height into the air was another matter.

She'd leave D'leer here, and she'd let her have her chance. She may well rouse before the Scitai could free themselves. Those people could be more than a day tied up on the floor.

She saw to Hectaro mounting up on Bastard, and she pulled herself up into Singer's saddle. She allowed herself a last look around the cavern.

"No way you make it out of Conflu," Tuppen called after her. "No one has *ever* gotten past our borders."

Lee happened to know for a fact the statement wasn't true.

They took back to the trail. Riding much lighter with proper saddle bags and food in their stomachs, they made better progress.

They were an hour away from the cavern before it occurred to Lee she should have made them tell her how much farther they had to go.

Deeper into the mountainscape now, the blue sky almost cloudless above them and the thinner air a little colder and a little more refreshing, the horses picked up a trot and Lee allowed herself a look around. The range rode from the north by northeast to the south by southwest. She could see where the trail wound down this mountainside to the west, crossed a tiny plateau full of trees and wound up another mountain.

There were mountains farther east, and no sort of plains past them. She didn't see a river or another city, but she knew they must be there.

She'd try to fly out there in her mind tonight if she could, but she had other worries now.

A few more hours and they were in the wooded plateau. It would be pointless now to cut brush and drag it from their horses because there was only one trail and they had to be on it. She worried there might be more Scitai but she didn't see any evidence and Karel of Stone had taught her the first sign of them would likely be an arrow protruding from her chest. It would be more in the nature of the Scitai she knew to let them pass by quietly and then either follow them or, more likely, report them, but she couldn't be sure of that, either. Now she could only be sure she stood in a wooded place, it was too soon to camp (as nice as it might be) and she needed to move on.

"Where – where are we?" Hectaro asked her,

He'd been sitting his horse fairly well for his drugged state, even at a trot. He seemed disoriented now, searching the wood with his eyes, turning around on his horse. Hectaro looked for all the world like he'd just woken up in someone else's bedroom, and Lee had to believe in many ways he had.

"What do you remember, Hectaro?" Lee asked him.

The woods gave them some shade. The day wasn't particularly hot, even though the sun had risen to its zenith overhead. The humidity after the rain storm still hung in the air, but it hadn't become sticky.

Lee's father had told her once, people loved to live in the mountains because there weren't many bad days, once you had a safe place to live and some food in your larder. Of course, food was the challenge.

"I remember – I remember..." Hectaro said, looking down and to his left. His hands fiddled with the reins. "I remember we were riding in the rain.

"And I remember finding... a cavern," he continued. "There were people – there were Scitai in it! They healed my leg. They took D'leer..."

Of a sudden he spun around on his horse, then turned to Lee, then looked around him.

"D'leer?"

Lee sighed.

"They captured us," Lee said. "The Scitai. They drugged us, they gave you bay root – not enough to kill you but enough to knock you out. They didn't waste it on me because they thought I was just a girl.

"I got us free, we escaped with more provisions and these saddle bags, but I couldn't get D'leer on your horse and I couldn't wait for you to recover. We had to go and I made the decision."

"You *left* her?"

"I *had* to leave her," Lee said. The look on Hectaro's face was telling.

She was a Wolf Soldier. She was a pack-mate to Hectaro.

He didn't want to leave her behind.

He looked back up the trail.

"No," she informed him. "Absolutely not."

"How far?" he asked.

"Too far," she argued. "Most of the day, right back into the teeth of them, while they're ready. They're Scitai, Hectaro. You won't be able to get within a daheer of their cave before you're riddled with arrows, and if they *do* leave you alive it will be to turn you over to the Confluni."

Hectaro fumed. She was right, and he knew it, but ingrained in every Wolf Soldier is to never leave one behind.

"Your *father* would go back," he said, finally.

Cheap shot, is what her father would say, Lee thought. "My *father*," she said, aloud, "would have lifted her onto the back of a horse. My *father* wears a man's weight in armor and carries a sword I've seen smash through a stone wall.

"My *father* wouldn't have been laying drugged on the floor and left me to save him and, if he had, my *father* would have thanked me."

Cheap shot right back to you, she congratulated herself.

Hectaro straightened and pulled on Bastard's reins. For a moment Lee thought he might go back to spite her, but he touched his heels to the stallion's ribs and sent him father down the trail, away from the cavern.

Lee followed quietly. She felt a lot of guilt over leaving D'leer behind, but there was nothing for it. The Uman couldn't be saved.

People died in war, and the Eldadorian Empire happened to be at war right now.

***

The daheeri dragged on, the sun crossed the sky as they travelled through the little plateau then up the far mountainside. Lee felt horribly exposed and kept looking behind her, expecting to see Scitai scurrying after them, firing their arrows. Instead she saw nothing – which came as no surprise, either. The Scitai weren't stupid – they would wait for the sun to go down before they tried anything, if they followed the two of them at all.

The stopped every few daheeri and watered the horses and refilled their bladders. When darkness settled they found a round, circular clearing on the trail with a fire pit to one side and evidence in the form of a cloth mat and some straw of someone bedding here a long time ago under an overhang of rock.

Hectaro was off his horse and had his fingers in the bedding while Lee scanned the mountainside, first with her eyes and then with her magic, sniffing out the tell-tale signs of living things, looking for their heat, listening for their noises.

Nothing at all – barely anything bigger than a mouse or a small bird. If the Scitai were following her, they were staying out of the range of her magic, and seeing as they couldn't know how far her magic might stretch, then they would likely stay pretty far behind.

"This is old," Hectaro said, unnecessarily. "Almost four months – they must do a caravan at the beginning and the end of the season – the rock is stained from older straw matting crushed under newer."

Lee didn't think Hectaro had been trained as a tracker, so he was relying on his intelligence and his reason, not his training. He might be wrong but Lee didn't think so.

"We can stay here, then," she said. "Hobble the horses, I'll pull our provisions. There's a fire pit over there and it has a chimney, but I don't think we should have a fire."

"No," Hectaro agreed. "We don't need to cook. We need to sleep."

They used the fire pit to keep their saddles and their provisions off of the ground, and they covered them with their leather hide. Lee fed grain to the horses and Hectaro had already moved them to the little graze there was available. They ate their own jerked meat and Hectaro sniffed around the provisions Lee had taken – dried fruit and poached chicken wrapped in leaves and herbs.

"Have you checked this?" he asked.

She looked up from the hunk of jerked meat she'd been gnawing on. They were sitting under the overhang, their backs to the rock wall, looking out over the edge of the trail to the far mountains, framed by the dying sun. The sky had turned red and the clouds were few.

"Checked it for what?" she asked.

"For bay root, or some poison?" Hectaro said. "This could be prepared for intruders or bandits."

Lee snorted. "In *Conflu*? I think not."

"I'm sure Conflu has thieves in it, just like Eldador," Hectaro insisted. "Is that something you can do?"

Lee had to consider. *Could* she do it? There were spells to keep food from spoiling, but to detect poison? Certainly there were, but she couldn't think of one, or of a similar spell she could experiment with.

"I haven't learned enough," she said.

Hectaro sighed. "Can you take the first watch?" he asked.

That surprised her.

"Look," he said, "I'll sample the meat, and if it puts me to sleep, then I'll just sleep while you watch, and you can wake me up when the moon is high. Otherwise we'll know it's safe."

Lee looked down, then back up at him. "I've never stood a watch before coming to Conflu," she said, finally. "I – I don't know what to do."

Hectaro's grinned his handsome grin. "It isn't a big deal," he said. "You stay awake, you keep your ears and eyes open, and you watch down the trail. This is a good spot – you're going to be able to see anyone before they see you. Don't waste your magic – people have been standing watch without it for years."

Lee nodded. Of course, if the food were drugged then she'd be alone to defend them, and if it were poisoned Hectaro might be dead. She'd try to heal him but healing someone who was poisoned wasn't the same as healing an injury.

Without another word, Hectaro took a nibble of the poached chicken. He ate a little of a dried apple next, and then he ate some peas and carrots.

He didn't die or get sick, so they'd eliminated poison.

He stretched out on a pair of horse blankets, putting his hands behind his head.

"Anything?" Lee asked him.

"Nah," he said. "I think I'm fine. I'm going to drift off to sleep."

Lee nodded, setting back to a place where she could see down either direction on the trail.

Another new experience, she thought to herself.

"Lee?" Hectaro called out to her, as the sun finally set and the darkness washed over them.

"Yes?"

"Thank you," he said, finally. "Thank you for rescuing me, for being there for me, for taking charge, which I know is hard."

"We all serve," Lee said, a common expression among the Wolf Soldiers.

In its entirety, "We all serve the Emperor, each in our own way."

"You served well," Hectaro said, "and I understand you had to leave D'leer. She was sworn to protect you and she let you down – she got no better than she gave you, except you would have saved her, had you been able."

Lee couldn't be sure in her mind, but she didn't argue, either.

***

It was almost an hour before Hectaro's soft snoring told her he'd fallen off to sleep.

A big part of standing watch involved long bouts of boredom broken up by nothing. The seconds didn't pass for what seemed like long minutes. For a while she sang herself little songs in her mind, but she bored of it. When she was confident her eyes had adjusted, she stood up and she padded around in her cloth-wrapped feet, making sure she didn't come near the edge of the trail, keeping away from the horses so they didn't neigh and didn't spook.

When exploring no longer entertained her, she looked to the moon in the sky, gauged its position and decided she was barely half way through her watch.

How did people *do* this? she wondered. It was insufferable. And to do it night after night, every night? She didn't envy the life of the Wolf Soldier guards who'd stood outside of the entrance to the Imperial nursery every night of her life. She'd never given them a second thought when she'd marched past them to bed, and then seen them in the next morning.

She wouldn't make the same mistake again.

Finally she walked a little way down both sides of the trail and used a little magic to assure herself no living thing was creeping up on them. A mountain fox surprised her for its proximity, watching her from a burrow under a rock alongside the trail. Some people tried to tame foxes like dogs but it rarely worked and then only when they started with a kit, not a full grown wild animal. She thought she might throw it a piece of their chicken but then it would do nothing but assure the animal it could rob them for food.

Foxes were wily – in fact, her brother's Andaron name, *Agtani Chewla* meant *clever fox*. A fitting name for the son of a man called 'White Wolf' by the Andarons.

She missed the little boy who'd been her shadow for the last seven years of her life. He'd been blooded – she'd seen the evidence herself. He'd become a man now – as his sister, it was time to give him a warrior's name. An Andaron sister names her brother as part of their tradition.

She spent a good many hours considering good ones.

***

She managed not to fall asleep, and woke Hectaro to take his turn at watch. She stayed awake long enough to make sure he didn't fall back asleep, then she laid down in the warm spot where he'd slept.

It smelled like horses, but it smelled to her a little like him, too.

Lee Mordetur had thought she would marry the Duke's son, Hectaro, some day. She'd fantasized they'd go on great adventures as her parents had, where they'd fight great enemies, he with his sword and she with her magic. How ironic they had gone and done just that.

Thinking these thoughts, Lee found sleep under a starry sky, high up in the mountains in a foreign land, watched over by the last of her Wolf Soldier guard.

Chapter Fifteen

More and Less Familiar

Their life was the same for a week. They woke, they rode while there was sunlight, then they found a place to rest and they took turns at watch. They woke the next day and they did it all again. One night it rained and they huddled under the leather tarp with their supplies, staying dry except for a trickle of ground water running down the incline they tried to sleep on.

At first they talked at length, about the things they dealt with as the children of royals, about D'leer, about their fathers and the campaigns they'd been on, about the things they wanted in their futures.

By the fifth day they'd had the conversations they could have. The scenery barely changed and the conversation mellowed with it. On the third night Lee realized the fox she'd seen was following them, and from then on she looked for it when she stood watch.

A fox should be skittish, however this one was almost friendly. On the fourth night she couldn't resist feeding it a few strips of jerked beef, the first one thrown to it and the third right out of her hand. She felt its needle-like teeth against her palm without it biting her, and for a quick moment she worried she would catch its diseases.

But that didn't happen, and then it became her constant companion at night. On the night of the sixth day, it crawled under the leather sheet with her and slept curled up against her stomach, her body curled up to bring her knees up against it.

In the morning Hectaro pulled back the leather sheet and the fox leapt to her defense, hissing at him with its hackles up.

Hectaro pulled his sword, Lee leapt to this little friend's defense.

"Lee – what? What are you doing?" Hectaro spluttered.

Lee stroked the fox's back. It almost snapped at her, then settled in at her side, looping once between her legs as she stood, rubbing its body against her like a cat.

"You've made a *pet* of that thing?" Hectaro demanded.

Lee shrugged. "I noticed it our first night out," she said. "It's been following us since the cavern."

"Have you been feeding it?"

Lee looked away.

"Not at first…"

Hectaro sighed. "We have to kill it, Lee," she said. "A fox isn't a clean animal – it will raid our food stores –"

Lee straightened. She reached her hand down and the fox turned its nose up and licked the ends of her fingers.

"If wanted to raid our food stores, it would have," she said. "You'll leave it be."

"They carry the water fear –" he argued.

Lee knew and she'd worried about it. The water fear was a maddening disease animals could contract from bites or eating the infected dead. They could pass it to any of the Fovean races. If infected, the person or the animal went mad, wouldn't eat, wouldn't drink, would become a snarling, drooling animal itself and then eventually die.

Foxes were scavengers and were usually the first sign of some animal dying of that disease, because they would eat its dead body.

"This one doesn't have it," she said. "It might be someone else's pet already, or just be hungry and alone. I don't know, Hectaro, but it's sweet and it's under my protection, and I accept responsibility for it."

Hectaro sighed, his frustration obvious. He knew he answered to Lee Mordetur, however he knew he had to protect her as well. The nobility had to know a lot about farming, and farmers wouldn't tolerate foxes.

Lee feared Hectaro would wait for an opportunity to kill the fox, then throw its body over the nearest cliff. The thing was trusting and wouldn't be hard to kill.

He started packing their stores. The fox stopped licking her fingers and trotted off down the trail, disappearing where the trail took a turn. They'd camped at a peak on the trail, where it widened, which is what they always tried to do. They didn't seem to have been followed by the Scitai but they might be, or they might find other guardians on the pass.

Lee saddled their horses. They'd developed this rhythm. In a short time they were mounted and moving to the east, chewing their jerked beef and eating a hand full of dried fruits or vegetables.

They turned the corner the fox had turned and it was nowhere in sight. Lee looked for it and couldn't see where it had gone. It did this – becoming almost invisible in the day, skulking where ever things like this skulked.

"It's gone," Hectaro commented. He seemed almost relieved.

"It will be back," she told him.

He frowned and they moved on in silence, save for the horses' hooves on the trail.

An hour later they found another wooded plateau at the bottom of their trail, where they could see the path rising up on the other side into the scrubby heights of another mountain. Trees sprung up nobly to either side, casting shadow from the hot, summer sun. White and brown bark, mostly smooth, stood out under giant boles, some dripping with dew left over from the chill mountain night.

The entered it as they had before. These areas usually had a trough for drinking water, and they could water the horses and refill their bladders. If there was a pool, Lee wondered if she might sneak a bath. The temperature dropped ten degrees in the shade and Lee noticed it. At the same time she noticed the skin on her arms had been browning. Dressed in what were little more than rags now, she likely looked a proper Andaron, except her hair was brown instead of black.

Their horses stepped under the canopy and began snorting. Bastard stopped and pawed the ground.

Lee raised a hand white with power, Hectaro pulled his sword. The animals always knew first.

Three Scitai stepped out of the trees with their cross pistols pointed at Hectaro. Once again they saw the girl and not the threat.

Lee could snap their bow strings if they were all in range, but if some were hanging back and she didn't get them, then those Scitai would know and they would fire immediately. Her mother might have shielded them from the Scitai arrows, but Lee didn't know how.

"I think you'll be stepping down from those great beasts," a bearded Scitai said. He was dressed in a white blouse like the ones worn by the last group of Scitai, and the same brown pants.

"I think I'll ride you down instead," Hectaro said.

"Will cost you your horse," the Scitai informed him.

"I think you plan to take him anyway," Hectaro answered.

Three more Scitai stepped out. Lee heard a rustle in the bushes. She realized what Hectaro was doing – risking his own life to bring them in, knowing what she could do.

Risking Bastard's life. Hectaro loved that horse.

Lee unfocused her eyes. The Scitai said, "One last warning."

She focused her will, this time she bore down on the spell, used her growing power, extended the reach of the magic.

The strings in the cross-pistols snapped. The bearded Scitai swore and threw the useless weapon aside, reaching into what seemed to be a pocket in the leg of his pants.

Hectaro drove his heels into Bastard's sides, Lee did the same. Both horses lurched forward.

Bastard had been trained as a war horse, and a war horse rode down the things in its way. Singer had not, she was a horse for pleasure riding. She lined up behind the stallion, as her instinct told her to do.

There was a sick crunch, and then a scream cut off in the middle. Singer stepped in what could have otherwise been slop on the road, slipped and righted herself. Six more Scitai leapt out of the bushes, reaching for other bows and finding the strings to those broken as well.

The horses ran on, through the woods, out the other side and up into the trail up the mountain. The Scitai were scrambling behind them. They were deadly with their arrows. If they managed to string one, this might turn out not to be an escape.

Turning in her saddle, Lee cast back not at the Scitai but at the trees around them. Three, then six, then ten of the mighty boles exploded into flame, raining down burning leaves and spewing smoke to obscure hers and Hectaro's escape up into the mountains. The Scitai would have to decide what they wanted to do more: kill invaders or preserve their home. Knowing Karel of Stone, Lee didn't doubt which they'd choose.

She and Hectaro charged up the path, and Lee couldn't help wondering if they hadn't found the ones who'd tamed the fox.

Chapter Sixteen

Down in a Hole

This part of the trail was covered in loose rock. Pressing up the mountain on the far side of the plateau, the stink of smoke rising up behind them, their horses' hooves slipped and Singer started to fall behind Bastard, who pushed out with both back hooves and took the incline in longer hops.

Lee felt tempted to call out to Hectaro to slow down but didn't. Sometimes climbing up an incline this steep, a horse needed to keep its momentum or start sliding back, and then could panic. She'd catch Bastard eventually – the path only seemed to be bound for one place.

Lee imagined she could hear the Scitai in hot pursuit behind them, however she knew pursuit was unlikely. Scitai loved their forests - they were inherently woodland creatures and carved their homes out of the living hearts of their trees, growing them over long generations. They'd leave the little people daheeri behind them before those fires were out, and would keep moving faster than a running Uman could pursue them, much less a stubby-legged Scitai.

Bastard topped the rise ahead of her. He should have stopped but didn't. When climbing a mountain there could be series of false peaks before the actual top, and might be what she was seeing now. Singer was making consistent progress up the mountainside, and Lee didn't press her. She'd get where she was going.

When she did several minutes later she was rewarded by a panoramic view of the eastern portion of the Confluni Empire – a city even larger than the one they'd left behind on the other side of the mountain pass, laid out onto the plains and, a few daheeri to the east, the banks of a mighty river running to the southeast and out of sight.

The plains were dotted with crops laid out in a patchwork of different shades of greens, yellows and reds. Even from this height, easily three daheeri above the city, she could see the Confluni workers scurrying between the city and the fields.

She could see blue skies overhead with only a few puffy clouds. The afternoon sun beat warm on her face and the smells of a city, the rank scent of people against the rich smell of growing things, rose up on a trade wind to meet her.

What she didn't see was Hectaro, not anywhere. The trail descended on a subtle incline, criss-crossing down the mountain. If he were on the trail she'd see him and, more importantly, the occupants of the city below would catch him easily before he made it to the ground. The journey down would take an entire day on horseback and was too treacherous for night travel. The unguarded turns would eventually catch even the most careful traveler. The path's existence was its own security for the city against an uninvited guest.

Hectaro wasn't on the path, and she could see no other. Beside it was loose rock and dirt, scrub brush which looked like it would give away if someone tried to rely on it to cross the mountainside horizontally. She'd overrun Bastard's hoof prints with Singer's however she could tell even with her novice skills that Bastard hadn't travelled down the incline.

She backed Singer up out of sight of the city and turned her around, then dismounted. She could see the divots from Bastard's pushing himself up the incline, but as the ground started to level off those were gone, and of course she'd run Singer right in the larger horse's path. She looked for a false entry in the cliff wall to her right and found nothing, however when she steeled her courage and peered down the mountainside to the depths below, she didn't see the signs of a fallen horse.

It was as if Adrian himself had taken Hectaro in the palm of His hand and brought horse and rider past the great beyond. Nothing else explained what had happened.

More than ever since this journey began, Lee wanted to cry.

**

An hour later she felt no better and knew no more. Singer called out to Bastard and there was no return neigh. Lee herself wasn't so bold. She used her magic to sharpen her sight and saw nothing different – what she could make out of the horse tracks seemed to just end abruptly.

Whatever had happened, it was still happening, and Hectaro was lost and most likely getting farther away from her. She needed to find him, which meant she needed to take some risks.

She tied her horse's reins to a stout root growing out of the mountainside. As she did this she wondered where such a thick root could be coming from. The mountain wall rose straight up another thirty men's heights or more without a break, and there was no source for this root to be coming from. Enough time later to discover this secret, though.

She sat on the ground and she pressed her back against the wall. She took two deep breaths to steady herself and she unfocused her eyes, thinking once again about the stables at the palace and, more specifically, about the hay in the loft.

When her brother had been five and a particular nuisance one day, she and he had decided to explore their parents' bedroom and to see if their mother had left anything interesting in there to get into. They'd looked through the armoire and all of the drawers in all of the dressers and found nothing more entertaining than a house mouse and a collection of daggers. Eventually her brother had crawled under the bed, and when he'd emerged he bore a huge grin on his face.

He'd opened his tiny palm and revealed a single gold Tabaar, the coin of the realm, this one with old King Glennen's face on it. Glennen had been King before her father and although she had supposedly met the man she had no memory of him. This coin may well have been laying under that bed for her entire life.

"Treasure!" Vulpe had exclaimed, and with the creativity of children they had become pirate adventurers reaping wealth from the land on the points of their swords. For years afterwards they'd found 'treasure' throughout the palace, a copper penny here or silver Tabaar there, rarely anything as good as that one fat gold coin, and they'd collected their wealth in an old wooden box their mother had given Lee to put her jewelry in, which she'd never gotten around to actually accumulating.

They'd hidden the jewelry box in the back of the hay loft, behind a false board where they'd cut the wall themselves with a hoof pick. On occasions when new hay had replaced the old or the eaten, they'd dug themselves tunnels and buttressed them with scraps of wood to give themselves passage to their buried treasure.

She hadn't seen that box in nearly a year. The game had grown stale and life's realities, alongside her budding infatuation with Hectaro, had replaced it. As far as she knew, however, the box was still where they'd left it, unless a stable hand had relieved them of it and they'd not known.

It would be a difficult summoning, which is what she needed for what she wanted to do.

She imagined that box, how it felt in her hands, how the wood smelled just a little musty, how the coins inside would rattle. She remembered the rough edges where they'd scored the board concealing it, the smell of the hay all around them, and the look on her brother's face when he'd hold that box in his hands and look up at her, waiting for her to create the new game.

She pushed that last thought away, and she summoned the box to her.

Her being soared out of the mountains, leaving her body behind. She could see the tree line several days' travel past, the plains, and then the rough paths travelled by Confluni National Guard to keep the forest secure. She saw the water of Tren Bay, blue and sparkling under the sun, gentle waves lapping the shores of Conflu.

And this time she turned around and looked back at the mountains, and as she willed the box to her, she returned back along the path, back over the city, and she studied the mountains for Hectaro and Bastard.

She didn't know how long she'd have to do this. She sensed she'd also found the box and it was beginning its journey to her. Like an ethereal eagle her being swooped back down to the mountain path, along the trail they'd yet to cross, looking for evidence, looking for clues, looking for some sign of her Wolf Soldier companion.

Nothing – there was simply nothing to see. In order to get more of a perspective she rose higher still, searching more land, allowing for the impossible event that she'd passed him or that he'd found some side trail and doubled back.

As she rose higher she could see what she thought was a mountain was in fact a dormant volcano, and what she'd thought must be its peak above her was instead the upper edge of a great chasm on its other side. She remembered the root she'd tied her horse to, and she investigated.

There she found him – the horse hobbled on a flat spot along the inner slope, too steep for any one person to climb. Once again she saw the Scitai, a dozen of them now, and Hectaro stripped of his clothing, tied wrists and ankles and laying on his side with a gag in his mouth. The Scitai were arguing, and one central among them seemed to be directing the others and trying to bend them to her will.

Another woman and, in this case, another sorceress. Her aura stood out clearly to Lee, red and powerful. This woman had the power either to translocate or to levitate rider and horse into the chasm and to do it quickly. She couldn't hear their voices but she could tell by their demeanor that they meant Hectaro no good.

Of a sudden, the box was in her hand, and she with it was returning to her physical body. There she was surprised to find her friend the fox curled up in her lap, its chin on her knee, its keen eyes clearly watching her as she approached. She swooped in and the fox straightened, its wise eyes looking right into hers, as the box plunked down on the ground before her, and her being sought her body.

She wasn't prepared for the fox's entity to meld with her own body, but in an instant she was a thing with four paws, sharp teeth, and sharper vision, smelling smells she'd never dreamed existed and laying in the lap of the girl whom something told her she was born to be with.

And if *that* wasn't a new sensation, Lee the fox didn't know what was?

Chapter Seventeen

More Familiar

How could she be *the fox*?

New smells filled her nose, making the end twitch. Everything looked sharper, but all of the colors were different. As a fox she could hear a mouse scurrying part way down the mountainside, and the shifting gravel moved by its passage.

She leapt off of her own lap and could see her body staring into nothing, her unfocused eyes blinking, her chest rising and falling with long, shallow breaths. She'd lost weight on this trip. Her hair was longer and shaggier than she remembered it.

She didn't know how long she'd be a fox, but she felt as if she needed not to waste this opportunity.

Her mind informed her she could find a crack in the mountainside only a few fox-lengths down the path, and she trotted down to it. Coordinating the movement of four paws seemed natural to her. Keeping a low center of gravity, focused on her middle, seemed natural as well.

Realizing that, as a fox, she had become male, seemed not only extraordinarily uncomfortable but filled the back of her mind with a whole set of urges which she could barely understand and certainly had no use for, and she did the best she could to push away and out of her consciousness.

She found the fissure in the rock wall. Her mind told her it was far too narrow for her body to squeeze through, however her memory spoke otherwise, and she squeezed into the crack and through it, feeling sharp rocks, dust and pebbles clinging to her luxurious fur coat and stinging the pads of her paws. She could smell a nest of mice she'd raided just the other day, replaced by a fresh one. Before she could stop herself she hit the nest and had a fat mouse crunching between sharp teeth. The mouse squealed as it died and the warm, salty taste of its blood flowed over her tongue and down her throat. She crushed the mouse's bones and swallowed it as the others scurried away.

She sniffed the nest for young and found none. Part of her was disappointed – the young mice were sweet – but she herself had no desire to experience devouring them.

She pressed on without another thought. Her sharp eyes picked out the path, avoided a hole in the fissure which would have sent her plunging deep into the volcanic remains beneath her, and found light at the end of the tunnel. An instinct she didn't know she had left her creeping the last few fox-lengths to the end of the fissure, pressing out the end of her nose first, sniffing for the dogs or other animals that bipeds often kept to guard the places where they lived and, finding none, creeping forward to invoke her eyes, to see what might be going on in the light.

She saw the Scitai which, as a disembodied woman, she'd seen from above. She saw Hectaro bound naked not 30 fox-lengths from her. She smelled but couldn't see Bastard, the musky stallion, and remembered the animal had tried to stomp her before.

She focused on the Scitai – they were the danger. She'd avoided arrows from them in the past, but barely. If she ran upwind of them, they'd smell her. Her human mind was surprised by this. As a fox she knew Scitai were more closely matched to foxes than any of the other bipeds this animal had encountered.

She recognized the sorceress among them – a powerful witch whose aura spoke of a connection to the goddess Weather. She commanded these Scitai to gather together, to get ready to find the woman who'd travelled with this Man.

They were focused on their weapons and their supplies. She knew she could slink over to Hectaro. They didn't have a dog.

She left the fissure and trotted first to a clump of brush growing out of the mountainside, then to a divot behind some rocks where Scitai had been relieving themselves, then to a pile of clothes which smelled of Hectaro, finally behind Hectaro himself.

By this point the Man had noticed her fox-self, but the Scitai had not. She pressed her fur to his body, behind him, and poked her head over his hip and watched them, ready for a headlong sprint back to the fissure, but nothing.

Out of a habit she didn't know she had, she made sure her escape path was secure. It was.

She found the rope binding the man's wrists, and she chewed it with her needle-sharp teeth. Chew, chew, chew, then check the area and make sure she was unnoticed. Chew, chew, chew and check again. A clever fox, she knew, was completely aware of its surroundings, or became part of a coat!

Lee realized she was already becoming more the fox and less the girl. She needed to stop doing this very soon, even though she wasn't entirely sure how.

Snap! The ropes binding the Man's wrists broke. She popped her head back up and saw the Scitai gathered around the sorceress again. They would be moving soon.

Of a sudden she realized she could be back in her body in an instant, if she wanted. There was no mystery to this magic – in fact, the fox was trying to shake her off from its person and take back its own mind.

She did so. The fox shook its head, and like a flea in its ear she was flung back through the mountainside, and Lee was a young lady sitting on the cold stone path, her butt sore and her legs tingling from blood loss, folded before her.

***

What should have drained Lee left her feeling more powerful than ever. She'd experienced a wild animal – her mother had told her only one in one hundred Sorceresses ever attracted a familiar, however she had, and it was the fox. Right now her fox was in grave danger, having gone into the lair of Scitai to save someone close to her.

With more of her being than she would have thought possible, she yearned for her fox, her familiar, a little friend more important than any other, more important even than a child could be to her in some ways.

A mountainside stood between her and it – and she had no knowledge of how to push through its depth or how to fly over it to get to her charge. A part of her mind still remembered that her furry friend knew his way back to her. Hectaro had untied his ankles and gone sprinting for his sword, leaving the fox unguarded, exposed, and vulnerable. She knew the Scitai would kill it if they could.

The sorceress called on the power of Weather, but Lee's connection to the fox reminded her how her power came from the god Earth, the wounded god, and things from Earth gave her power.

She reached out into the mountain wall between them, she felt the essence of it, the rocks and dirt and sand in it, and she willed it to disperse.

It resisted her and she bore down. She reached into it, she shook it, she twisted it with her mind.

The rock wall groaned, shuddered, and then shattered into a million, million pieces. Singer reared and called out. Bastard answered her.

A 'V' in the rock wall appeared before her. On the other side of the mountain pass, the Scitai were already scrambling for their weapons and their sorceress was calling on her power.

***

Lee had never sparred with another sorceress, not even her mother. Lee saw the other's aura through her being rather than her eyes. The Scitai woman was furious and was calling on powers born of her emotions.

The sky overhead roiled, the clouds darkening and obscured the sun.

She'd call on lightning. Predictable.

It probably wasn't the best time for the Scitai in general to be standing on an inactive volcano, Lee thought, grinning.

Hectaro sprinted naked for the Scitai warriors, his sword swinging low. They drew their bows back as one, picking him out.

Lee broke their strings. Beneath them, the volcano shifted.

The sky above them roiled.

The fox bolted through this new chasm in the rock wall and bounded past her, leaping for Singer's saddle and scrabbling up into the seat.

Singer called out again, and Bastard bolted after the fox.

Thunder rolled. The ground shook. Hectaro killed one surprised Scitai male holding a broken bow, and then the woman behind him.

Lee felt ten daheeri tall inside of herself, her power swelling, the wounded god feeding her beneath her feet, feeding her power through the mountain itself. The rising wind caught her hair and whipped the ends.

Thunder rolled again. The mountain shook.

Hectaro killed again, another woman. The Scitai were scattering.

The Scitai sorceress raised her hand. She'd call the lightning.

Lee called for an eruption from the dormant volcano beneath her. She realized almost as she did it that the force of the blast would kill them all.

She didn't care.

Lightning struck! She felt its energy crash down at her. She rooted herself to the god Earth, to his living skin as rock and sand beneath her, and the energy passed through her to Him, then back to her as renewed power.

She stamped her foot and the ground shook. A shockwave resonated from her as she drove her heel into the ground and directed its might at the Scitai woman who'd defied her.

The other sorceress made a scooping motion and pulled the energy from Earth and threw it to the four winds, sending it north, south, east and west, feeding the turmoil in the sky, bringing more thunder, calling more lightning.

The raw energy struck Lee. She directed it back to Earth and it was returned to her, more might than she had ever in her life experienced.

This would burn her essence out if she continued. This would give her the black mind. The sorceress was more powerful than she and had clearly battled before. Lee could only pull attacks out of her imagination. This sorceress had been trained and had survived battles.

The mountain shook for the lava called up from beneath it. They would soon experience Earth's raw might, and none would survive.

Rain began to fall. The wind whipped it against her, against the horses. Bastard and Singer were rearing and snorting. The fox clung to her saddle with long, sharp claws.

Hectaro struck again and again, naked, blood covering him, the rain painting his skin, making a bizarre mural on his body.

Lee saw this and she had her answer.

She took her new power and she called down the rain alongside the sorceress. She mixed it with the Earth, she made mud.

She made it at the sorceress' feet, called it deep, pulled it up and shaped it like a claw and struck at the sorceress. The other called on more rain to her, to wash it away, Lee added more raw earth to it.

Hectaro spun around, looking for more Scitai, and his eyes found her. Lee was marginally aware of his seeing her, of his seeing the fox and their horses.

She couldn't call to him without breaking her focus on the other sorceress, but the fox was not so encumbered. The animal leapt from Singer's back and bounded quick as a wink back through the chasm and to the warrior's side. He raised his sword and then recognized it, the little creature who had freed him.

The sorceress called down more lightning, trying to overwhelm Lee. Lee cycled it into the ground beneath them, where lava roiled and the dirt and rock had begun to shift, begun to clear a channel beneath them.

The eruption she was calling would be gigantic.

Hectaro sprinted for his horse, the fox leading the way. The sorceress had sunk to her hips in the mud beneath her. Lightning hammered down on Lee.

Hectaro sprinted past her and plunged his sword into her back. The woman screamed.

The sky above them exploded into a frenzy of rain and lightning. Strikes surrounded them randomly, crashing into the mountainside and even into the city beneath them. Avalanches began as the lightning struck peaks to either side of them and the path below.

Lee felt staggered by the sudden victory. Her knees buckled and she felt the sharp stone pierce her shin before she realized she'd fallen.

Hectaro scooped up his clothes and then sprinted through the chasm. The fox leapt past them both and then up into Lee's saddle on Singer's back.

The ground shook.

No matter what happened, Lee couldn't help thinking, it was going to be bad.

Chapter Eighteen

Down the Mountain

Lee had heard an expression from her father many times. "It's time to get the hell out of Dodge." She never understood that. What was Dodge? How do you get out of it? Was this a place or a state of being or some adult expression she wasn't privy to? He always said it when he wanted to leave some place and leave it as fast as he could.

Say what you would, she thought, taking a fist full of a nervously prancing Singer's mane, it was time to get the hell off of this mountain, and if tragedy made this mountain 'Dodge,' then she was fine with that.

"What – what's going on? What happened?" Hectaro demanded of her, hopping up and down into his Wolf Soldier britches, his boots and his shirt on the ground next to him.

"What's going on is we're standing on a volcano," Lee informed him, pulling herself up into the saddle behind the shivering fox. The animal pressed its luxurious fur up against her middle and took some of the fabric of her make-shift shirt in its teeth, probably for comfort. "What's about to happen is that it is about to vomit up a million tons of lava all over us, and what will happen after depends on how far we can be from here."

Hectaro's eyes went wide and he fastened his britches. He pulled his boots on with no stockings, took one longing look at his Wolf Soldier tunic and blouse, then leapt topless up onto Bastard's back, barely taking the time to aim the toe of his boot for the stirrup. The stallion reared half-way up to its full height as he settled into the saddle and took a short rein on the terrified animal.

"After me," he ordered her, and hammered his heels into the stallion's ribs. Bastard took off down the path without any other provocation.

Singer took off after him. Lee had no allusion as to her being able to keep up with Bastard. Nearly as fast as her father's Blizzard, Bastard would out-distance any other horse alive. If she could manage to keep him in sight, that would be quite an accomplishment.

Put him behind her, however, and he'd overrun the poor mare and maybe bump her off of the trail to get past her. In a headlong flight you lined up the horses in order of their speed, and the last one in line just had to suffer through as best as he or she could.

Lee also knew from her mother's training there was a time when you picked a path for your horse, and a time when you trusted in its instincts. Yes, a running horse could find a chuck hole or loose gravel, slip and fall and break a leg or worse. In fact, they'd been running from predators since the first foal emerged blinking on the first grassy plains, and by and large they had survived. They were smart enough to pick their way when they had to, and if they saw something they weren't sure of, they'd usually just leap over it.

Thundering headlong down the winding path from the mountain top, the very earth beneath their feet shuddering as the wrath of an awakened god stirred beneath them, Lee leaned forward, pressing her middle against the terrified fox, becoming one with her mount as much as she could. In front of her she could see Hectaro doing the same thing, already skidding around the first turn, Bastard's hooves slinging gravel out behind him.

Lee wanted to pull back on Singer's reins but didn't, and was gratified when the horse slowed on her own. She took the turn in the path and her hooves scrabbled for purchase, her back legs slipping out to her right for one terrifying moment before she righted herself and pressed on down the path. Behind and above them the volcano belched out a plume of ash into the blue, blue sky, and before and beneath them she heard a dozen screams rise up from the city below them.

She'd planned to do this at night, but felt fortunate this was happening during the day now. She'd hoped to prevent the people in the city from seeing them, but now she doubted they would care. She'd estimated it would take at least a day for them to get to the bottom, but as she could see Bastard already skidding to a stop to take a much-tighter second turn, she wondered if they wouldn't accomplish this in just a few hours.

Bastard would probably not be too far ahead of her until he hit the flat plains. The path was treacherous and already the powerful stallion was slowing, his natural caution and his fear of the height from the path's open edge over the ground weighing in against his fear of the volcano belching ash behind them.

They ran for another hour before the first white flakes of ash fell among them. They would be raining down on the city in a few moments, as well. Lee had never seen a volcano, really never thought much about them except as an anomaly of nature from her studies. One had not erupted in Fovea in her life time or in her mother's.

Her father, however, seemed well-familiar with them and spoke of them with a certain awe and terror. He had described the heat capable of melting stone, the ash falling in such quantity it could crush buildings, the waves of molten air that could strip the skin from a living thing with no more effort than she would peel the skin from a Toorian banana. He'd spoken of whole cities being buried and unearthed centuries later, some empty of people and some with the remains of those too foolish to get out of harm's way, clinging to each other in terror, or at rest where toxic gas or their own poisons had taken them moments before they were covered.

The whole thing had seemed incongruous and fantastic to her as a student. She'd listened to the stories more to be around her father and to hear his voice than because she cared what he had to say on the subject, but the information haunted her now.

Ahead of her, Bastard took a turn too wide and slid on his butt toward the edge of the path, her heart freezing in her chest as she waited to see the giant stallion fly sideways into the open air, to scream as it plummeted to its and to Hectaro's deaths on the rocky slopes beneath.

Hectaro leaned against the skid and pitched his weight, a fraction of the stallion's, back to the path. If that helped Bastard she couldn't tell, but the stallion with its back legs folded beneath him came to a stop less than a hand's breadth from the precipice, its black tail actually swinging into the open air, and then he leaped forward and ran back down the trail again, momentarily out of her sight.

She actually did slow Singer as she approached this turn. It was loaded with trap rock – loose gravel that would slide under hooves – and Singer had to pick her way across it at barely a trot. Once she'd covered that space and could point herself straight down the trail again, she sighted Bastard, now well ahead of her, and took off at a canter again, her hooves flying down the path.

The shivering fox reached its head up and licked the underside of Lee's jaw. Lee had to smile despite herself. *How had this little friend, this dear familiar, found her,* she wondered. *What would it mean to her life and to her magix to have it at her side?*

This stretch of the path was long and Singer stretched her body to its full speed. Ash was starting to interfere with their vision and there were moments when grey Bastard faded in and out of the white ash. Screams were coming more regularly from the city before and beneath them. She thought she might be able to see a stream of people collecting outside the city gates but she couldn't be sure. The ground gave a terrible shake and Singer stumbled and righted herself, propelling herself headlong down a path rapidly becoming harder and harder to see.

The ash would soon begin to interfere with their breathing. More importantly, the horses would breath of it while they exerted themselves, and they'd really suffer ill effects. There were things she could do to prevent this, but she needed to stop to do them, meaning she needed to get Hectaro to stop first.

She didn't even waste her time calling for him. As far ahead as he was, he'd never hear her over Bastard's shod hooves on the ground. Had this been her mother, she'd have just called out to her in her mind. She'd tried this with her father and her brother before, neither of them magically gifted, and her father claimed he could hear nothing of her thoughts no matter how hard she tried, and while her brother had sometimes claimed he could feel images from her, he was likely lying about it and could never tell her accurately what those images were.

She could disrupt the ground around the stallion to slow him, but that would be dangerous. She could make something explode before them but that might spook him or, even worse, damage the trail. She wracked her mind for something she might do to get Hectaro's attention and was in fact so distracted she nearly ran her horse into his when she came across him stopped on the trail.

Singer reared. The fox leapt to safety. Bastard snorted and pawed the earth, white flecks of ash already hanging from his black mane.

"Whoa!" Hectaro shouted at her. What was it about emergencies like this that made men shout? She shook her head – no time to argue about it now.

"Sorry! Sorry!" she shouted back at him, getting her mount under control. The fox circled them both, staying clear of Bastard. She remembered from her time as the fox how the stallion had tried to stomp him.

"This ash is no good," Hectaro informed her. "We're breathing it. The horses are breathing it."

Lee nodded. Hectaro had been trained in the same schools by the same people as she, her father included as one of his instructors.

"I have more cloths," she said. "We wet them, we tie them over our mouths and over the horses' noses."

Hectaro nodded and he dismounted, she after him. He took a firm hold on both skittish animals' bridles, keeping them facing each other so they wouldn't fight for space on the trail.

The fox actually brushed up against his leg and lay down across his boot, looking up at him, his teeth slightly bared. He looked for all the world like he was trying to smile.

"That thing saved me, you know," Hectaro commented as Lee unpacked the roll behind her saddle.

"Did it?" Lee asked him, pulling out the remains of her palace skirt.

She'd hated this thing. It was too bulky and hard to move in. When she sat it wanted to bunch under her, and it baked her on a sunny day.

But this dress had done a lot to keep her and her friends alive on this adventure, and she owed the dress maker an amazing bonus when she got back to Galnesh Eldador.

The ground shuddered and the ash fell a little more heavily. Above and behind them a red glow pulsated through the turmoil where the top of the volcano should be.

If she were to get there, she thought. Her mother would likely have a lot to say about the way she experimented with her newfound powers, as well.

Chapter Nineteen

Run for the Hills

From the bottom of the path they could see the city and the tilled fields around it. The yellow-skinned Confluni were milling through the fields. Others wearing armor and with swords over their shoulders and whips in their hands rode shaggy ponies and clearly kept them working with no more regard for the volcano erupting over them than for the sun setting to the west behind it.

"How can they still be working?" Lee demanded of Hectaro.

He shrugged. "The Confluni," he said, simply. "We don't know very much about them, but from the way they make war we know their leaders throw them at their enemies and either win or throw more. Maybe they just don't care that much about them?"

"Maybe they don't know that much about volcanoes," Lee argued, "or this happens more frequently than we think."

They spoke from behind wet cloths tied over their faces, but their skin had been colored first ghostly white, then streaked with black as the ash changed color. Their horses maintained long, wet strips of cloth covering their noses and mouths, hanging like beaks before them. They'd breathed a little of the ash and there was no avoiding that, but based on the collection of black at their nostrils on the cloth, they were being saved from a lot.

They'd already cleaned and soaked all of their cloths three times. Above them they could see a long, red worm of lava descending down the path. Lee had done this, she reminded herself, and she was going to end up hurting a lot of innocent people.

More if they weren't even going to try to run away.

"The sun will be down soon," Hectaro said, "and the ash will make it even harder for them to see us. We cut to the north, we press east until we're past this city, and when we're out of the range of the ash, we move as fast as we can for the river you said you saw."

Lee nodded. That was a good plan.

A good plan where they left a few thousand people to die.

***

Night fell, and the Confluni on their shaggy ponies herded the workers in the fields back into their city. The ground trembled regularly now and every hour or so a flaming red mass of rock came bouncing down the mountainside. Already the path behind them had been scored in a dozen places. Ash had stopped falling but they still wore the wet rags over their faces.

"We move," Hectaro informed her. He'd taken charge of the operation and she didn't fight him over it. There were things sorceresses did to lead their tribes and there were times when men trained in fighting battles took charge. To try to say *she* was the princess and *she* had to be the one giving orders would be ridiculous. Hectaro had proven his loyalty more than once.

She pulled herself up into Singer's saddle and the fox jumped up after her, its claws sharp in her lap and its head pressed against her stomach. Hectaro mounted Bastard and the much-larger stallion pranced, ready to run from here.

"We need to keep together," he informed her, "so I'll hold him back. We'll run side-by-side if we can and I want you to do that thing where you enhance your vision. Keep looking for men hiding – there will be deserters from the city, so there will be guards to catch them."

Lee nodded. She hadn't thought of that but it made sense.

They trotted out from cover and into the open. A blanket of ash suspended in the air above them hid the moon and stars. Lee tried to collect all of the light she could to see by, but the sky provided precious little.

She decided on something else instead. She let her mind flow into the ground around her, ahead and to either side, and she *felt* for other living beings. She looked for holes in the ground capable of tripping the horses, and for cattle-wire. She thought about how these things would feel if she could put her hands on them, what they might look like, what made them special.

At first she had nothing, then as if she'd discovered a whole new sense, she absorbed the characteristics of the local terrain.

They were trotting across a potato field. The land had been tilled but it was choked with ash now. She pressed Singer to her left, Bastard already giving way to the mare, when they came across a pile of hoes abandoned in the field. A little farther into the field they crossed a path and Hectaro decided they shouldn't follow it. It would be too obvious a place for guards to watch.

She pressed her mind out farther. It was more fields, more roots planted and growing. She informed Hectaro and they picked up a canter, the tilled soil muffling their horses' hooves.

They pressed on for a daheer before they came across a line of cattle wire and had to turn north. On the other side the aurochs were lowing and pawing, charging each other and testing the fence. Without warning two of them picked up their canter from the other side of the fence, herding with them, probably believing one running animal would guide them to the freedom they couldn't otherwise find.

"War's beard!" Hectaro swore. "Can you drive those things away?"

"I don't know anything about aurochs," she hissed back at him, wondering why he cared.

She found out soon enough when she heard a shout behind them, and heard the muffled beat of dozens of hooves. The aurochs had drawn the attention of the guards, and those guards had seen them. They had many daheeri to cross in order to find safety and this was too soon to be seen.

Nothing for it! Singer picked up her pace and Bastard matched it. They heard the Confluni shouting behind them in their own language – one she barely spoke. She recognized, "Stop!" and "Get them!" and something that was either a call for help, or a call to go get help. She moved her sense behind her and she could count six of the ponies which she assumed all had riders, already falling slowly behind.

She moved her sense back in front of her just time to prevent them from running into more of the barbed fence. One field ended and another began, leaving a channel in between that they could run through.

She was about to direct Singer into it when the aurochs hit it headlong. No less than four of them rammed the wire without slowing and were immediately entangled in its cruel barbs. One that had been following behind overran its fellows and managed to ram the fencing on the other side, and then there were half a dozen of them monstrous bovines kicking and screaming as they became more entangled in the fencing, obscuring their path to the east.

"West!" Lee shouted. That brought a chorus of challenges from the riders to the south, and she cursed herself for not thinking to give the order in Confluni. Now their pursuers knew they were chasing foreigners, rather than simple thieves! Hectaro cut Bastard sharply to his left and she followed, pulling Singer up alongside of him, between him and the fencing. She could tell this stretch ran for little more than a quarter of a daheer before it turned north.

And between that corner and them, five Confluni warriors lay stretched out on the ground, laying on their swords to prevent any light from betraying them, a practice of seasoned scouts for the Confluni National guard.

"Before us!" Lee hissed. "Five."

"Arrows?" Hectaro challenged her. Bowmen would have them before they could approach close enough for Hectaro to use his sword.

"I don't think so," she answered. Hectaro's sword sang as he pulled it from the sheath over his shoulder. He pushed Bastard out from Singer and the fence. She'd called this man a coward once, to his face, but she had to admire his courage now. Her own father would have hesitated to take on five to his one, encumbered by another to protect.

But then, his father had her mother, Shela, and now Hectaro had his own sorceress, too.

Where Shela might have killed them all with a thought, Lee softened the tilled soil beneath them. She called up the moisture in the soil from a dozen feet below them, and she made something simple into something profound.

The Confluni in attempting to leap to their feet and to surprise the horseman, instead found themselves mired in wet dirt. Some were fishing for their swords in an inch of mung while others slipped and fell. Lee hadn't had time to do much, but then she hadn't needed much, just to slow them down.

Hectaro was upon them and Bastard's hooves did the work his sword would have been hard-pressed to match. Lee shut her eyes and turned away as Singer followed, the living ground shuddering beneath her as her shod hooves crushed bone and drew muffled screams from the hapless Confluni guards.

Was this how her father felt when he made war? In the days after great battles, when his mood hung over him and those around him like a dark cloud, and her mother knelt beside him with her head in his lap and her long, black hair draped over a cushion beside him, he sitting on one of the couches in the Imperial residence, holding a cup in one hand and staring into the space before him, were these the sounds haunting him? Was this the guilt sucking the energy from his soul?

Lee could feel the guilt in her now as Singer pressed on, out of the blood, mud and broken bones and into open space beyond.

Bastard pressed on, Singer behind him, the Confluni warriors moaning into the mud. Behind them the other Confluni warriors on their ponies ran down their own without hesitating, finishing the pain Lee had started. The ponies had a harder time in the mud and lost a little more ground, and Lee pushed Singer to move faster.

When Singer gained on Bastard, the stallion picked up his pace. They approached the end of the cattle-wire fence and Hectaro would have ridden right past it, oblivious in the dark, had Lee not called out to him.

"To your *right*," she hissed. Hectaro wheeled Bastard to that side, skirting the corner wide, and Singer followed him. Lee pressed this new sense of the earth forward and tried to sniff out the next threat to them.

The darkness and the sulfur reek of ash pressed on them. The horses snorted, the wet rags over their noses slapping at their faces as they ran and upsetting them. Lee could smell the ash through hers, telling her all of their protection needed to be changed.

However she doubted the guardsmen behind them would give them the opportunity.

She pulled her horse back up alongside Bastard, between him and the fence as they cantered on. The ponies were still falling behind, but they'd taken the same turn she and Hectaro had. Either the guards had some magic of their own, or were guided by their own familiarity.

Either could help them.

"Faster," she hissed at Hectaro. Without answering, he picked up Bastard's pace and Singer matched him. The stallion could out-distance the mare but his speed didn't mean Singer wasn't a fast horse. Andarons were well known for their speed.

They covered half of a daheer and came across another right-hand turn. Lee sensed the ponies behind them, pushing hard, losing ground but not giving up.

They could out-distance the ponies, but probably not out-run them. There would be wide, flat terrain ahead, and the Confluni would be able to harass them for daheeri. If they were willing to press their mounts to death, then they could probably get close enough to threaten them, or they could send riders back for reinforcements, or might know some short-cut to get ahead of them. Whatever the circumstances, they were better off with the Confluni off of their tails.

She reined in Singer, Hectaro stopped Bastard just past her. She dismounted, the fox with her. She handed her reins to Hectaro and she ran to the fence.

Just the idea of doing this wrung her heart. The sound of the ponies' hooves barely reaching her ears, she stepped to the closest of the fence posts. Her will ran down four fence lengths. She put both hands on the bottom of the fence post where it touched the ground, and she focused her mind.

This was going to tax her. She didn't know how much energy she'd have left to sense their way, but she felt certain this was her last fight for a while.

She felt the base of the post shudder. Breaking the post would have been possible but taxing. Pulling all of the moisture out of it and making it brittle was a lot easier.

"Snap the post off," she ordered Hectaro, standing.

"I – I can't..." he stammered.

"Just do it," she said. She didn't have time to argue. The ponies were approaching.

Hectaro walked both horses to the fence. He took the top of the post in his hands and grunted as it broke off at the ground. Lee ran to the next post and did the same thing. "Pull the fencing out to the West," she told Hectaro as she squatted, reaching for the bottom of the next post.

He hooked his arm around the top of the post and kicked Bastard into motion. The horse knew the pain of barbed wire and shied from the post; Hectaro ended up dragging it on the horse's left side. Lee sucked the water out of the second post, then stood and took its top in both hands, rocking the post back and forth until the base snapped.

Hectaro kept pulling. She stayed to the north of the post and guided it as best she could while Hectaro kept moving to the west.

When she felt the wire tightening, she ran to Hectaro and ordered him, "Stop!"

She knelt at the bottom of the post he was holding and she softened the ground beneath it. The post sank a little and she hardened it.

Hectaro stepped Bastard and Singer away from the posts, to their north, and she followed, stepping away from the post and making sure it didn't move. It wouldn't be strong but in fact she wanted it to fall over.

This was a terrible thing to do to their enemy's innocent ponies, but they needed to escape.

"Ride," she ordered him. In less than a minute the ponies would overtake them. She ran for Singer, the fox bounding alongside of her, and she leapt up into the saddle. The fox jumped up into its usual place, taking her make-shift blouse in its teeth.

She put her heels to Singer's sides and the mare took off to the east. Hectaro caught up to her a moment later.

The cantered on, Lee trying as best she could to pick out the way before them. Moments later they heard the ponies scream, having run headlong without warning into the outstretched barbed fencing.

They wouldn't be going anywhere. In the dark it would take them a long time to untangle screaming ponies terrified by their own pain. They might end up putting them down and walking back.

They'd escaped, but Lee couldn't help feeling like she'd left a portion of herself behind.

In her mind, she told herself, "Today you earned the name Mordetur."

Chapter Twenty

A Student of History

They ran through the night. After an hour with no pursuit, they stopped and changed the wet rags they used to protect themselves and their horses. The air reeked of sulfur and ash. It covered their skin and their horses' hides. Ash clung on Lee's eyelashes and in Hectaro's hair.

When the dawn rose to the east, climbing up onto the plains, it revealed a sky red with spreading ash and an orange glow to the west which had to be the growing strength of an erupting volcano. Lee considered the consequences of wielding her magic so carelessly, merely because she could.

A lot of people were going to die because of her.

It weighed on her soul.

"What's wrong?" Hectaro asked her as they stopped. The horses were exhausted and Lee wanted to drop out of the saddle and sleep on the ground. In the last few days she'd exercised a lifetime of magic and felt weary in her bones.

"I'm tired," she said, almost moaning, her voice strange and hoarse to her own ears. "We all need to rest. We should find a place."

"Can you...?" Hectaro asked her.

But he was worried thinking she'd already pushed too hard, so he didn't know if he *should* ask. That aggravated her.

She wasn't a little girl.

She ran a hand through the fox's luxurious fur. He took her thumb in its teeth and held it gently. She had to admit the familiar helped her to channel more power, just as the teachings said. She'd have never hung on this long without it. She wondered if she took its power or if it were a conduit. It didn't seem as exhausted as she.

Lee unfocused her eyes, pushed her mind out into the earth around her, looking for something like the hollowed out hills they'd found to the West.

Nothing. She moved out farther, but the hills here were more rolling and less pronounced than on the other side. She found evidence of older roads several feet beneath the top layer of soil, and the foundations of old buildings. People had lived here once. This place had been more densely populated, but that must have been a long, long time ago, in the time of the Cheyak.

She was about to give up when she found an old, deep hollow in the ground, still sound.

"East," she said. "About four hundred strides."

They trotted the horses and found the place. The ground around them, lush with grass and some kind of weed or small flower with white petals and a yellow center, looked the same as anywhere else.

"Where?" Hectaro asked her.

It would take hours to dig, and they were exhausted. She felt the place out with her mind – the place she'd found seemed like some kind of basement with a strong roof above it, meaning a strong floor to some building that had been leveled a long time ago.

There had been a ramp so things could be moved in and out of it. She could sense its presence. There were doors that protected it, now one with the earth around it, creating a hollow.

She moved all of the moisture out of the dirt covering it. A wide space about eight feet by six became a depression a few feet to their east.

The effort left her semi-conscious in her saddle.

Hectaro ran to the spot and started to scoop away dirt with the consistency of sand from it. He didn't dig for more than a few minutes before it buckled underneath him. She'd destroyed the door with the earth.

She was too weak even to ask if he was alright.

He emerged comically, covered in sand and ash, looking like some giant gopher. He found a piece of wood that still remained strong and he used it to break a narrow channel free. In a few more minutes he had a passage and he led his own horse, then Singer down into it.

Lee wasn't even aware of when Hectaro pulled her from her horse and laid her down on a pile of horse blankets. She felt dimly aware when the fox curled up alongside of her, and Hectaro had fed it a piece of jerked meat.

Then all was black and quiet.

***

She awoke in the dark, unaware of where she might be. She lay on her side in a pile of horse blankets, the horse musk filling her nose. She felt a warmth at her stomach. She reached for it and felt the luxurious fox fur that was becoming more and more familiar for her. She felt the fox lick her finger, then take the tip of it in his sharp teeth.

She enhanced her eyesight and her stomach rumbled. The hunger pains were almost exquisite. She knew she'd need a moment if she planned to stand.

They were in some sort of dirty basement. Thick beams lined the ceiling, ten feet above her. Stout boards stood out on top of thick beams, hand cut, as much as six inches thick – what must have been a floor to a room above them. Old hooks hung from the rafters on chains, cobwebs still clinging to them. Dust and dirt lined the floor. The walls were piled rocks mortared together, but over the years they had leaked, and there were long channels down the walls and piles of mud turned to dirt up and down a room about fifty feet long and thirty feet wide.

The horses stood to one side. There had been hay piled up for them, wild-cut from the plains. Dirt had been piled up around them to contain their waste, and they'd been hobbled. Their saddles and tack hung on hooks from the ceiling, across from them.

Hectaro was nowhere to be found.

"Hectaro?" she whispered for him.

Nothing.

She sat up and scanned the rest of the room. She sensed the remains of a table or a counter on the far side. This might have been a cutting cellar for a slaughterhouse. It would stay cool here in the heat of the summer, as it was right now. The air smelled musty but not unpleasant. She must have slept through the day.

She didn't know what situation he might be in, and she knew better than to betray her warrior by calling out. She wanted to go to their packs and get food, but she didn't want to fall from her own weakness on the way.

She ran her fingers through the fox's fur, and then she pointed at the packs. She thought about him fetching back their meat pouch, and she projected that thought as gently as she was able to the fox.

He leapt up, trotted over to the pouches, dug around with his paws and then returned with its drawstrings in his teeth, the pouch dragging the ground behind him.

She took it, pulled the strings open, and picked out a decent piece and fed it to him. He laid down to chew it. She got herself a few large pieces and began to eat.

She felt energy flow through her body again. While she ate, she fed her magic as well. Satisfying her hunger and fulfilling her magic were becoming two separate sensations. Her mother had told her this before but she hadn't appreciated it until now. She wondered if Shela felt this way all the time. She wasn't shy about using her magic, and she'd seen her mother eat a man's portion after.

She ate more than she'd wanted to, and still no Hectaro. She stood and went to the packs herself, pulled out dried carrots and dried apples and ate them. She didn't feel guilty like the last time – now she appreciated the magic they were dependent on to survive. They'd gone farther than anyone would hope to in Conflu and had farther to go. They'd need her power.

She pushed her senses out into the ground around her. There were crushed buildings in all directions. Now that she had her wits about her she could detect levels of ash as well as dirt. This place had seen volcanic activity since these buildings had been built. Her father had told her ash from a volcano could crush a building. Now she thought how this must have happened here.

Maybe the city behind them was doomed.

Those people should have known better than to stay.

Past the buried city she found Hectaro by his feet on the ground. There was an antelope near him. He must be hunting it. She smiled to herself. She pulled moisture from the surrounding area to the dirt at the antelope's feet and felt the animal start to prance. It was standing in mud from nowhere and it didn't understand. It was distracted.

Lee screamed when the spear plunged through the antelope's heart. The fox jumped and started running a circle around her. She hadn't appreciated how she'd share the animal's pain this way. Before she could pull her mind away, she felt the animal stumble, the heart stop, the darkening to its eyes, the spreading pain of constricting lungs and arteries, moving from the chest to the body, to the brain.

A long, intolerable, unavoidable pressure as lungs stopped breathing, heart stopped beating, a sadness as she realized she'd never run the plains again, never be free, never see her mate, her younglings.

Her younglings!

And the antelope was dead. Tears flowed like rivers down her cheeks. The fox leapt into her lap and licked at them. It sensed her pain and didn't know what to do. She hugged the animal close, weeping, rocking it, trying to forget what she'd experienced with the antelope.

A sorceress knew death better than any other. Her mother had told her and Lee had assumed it was a comment on her mother's fierce reputation as one of the most formidable sorceresses of her time.

She knew different now.

***

She collected herself before Hectaro returned, the antelope's meat wrapped in its skin and that skin used as a satchel which he carried over his shoulder. He saw her sitting and he smiled.

"Good morrow, my Lady," he said. "I trust you're refreshed?"

"Refreshed enough," she said. "When do we get going?"

He laughed out loud and set the skin down. The fox ran to it and he shooed it away. It skirted him and sat back, waiting for an opening to raid the spoils.

He sighed, pulled out a long, fatty strip of meat and threw it to the fox, who took it and ran out of the cellar through the entrance Hectaro had dug.

No light came from there. That hadn't occurred to Lee. It wasn't day, it was night.

"How – how long?"

He squatted down and began to separate the meat on the skin. "All yesterday," he said. "All last night, and today. The sun went down about two hours ago."

She started to get back up. "We need to leave," she insisted.

He stood and crossed the short distance between them, putting his hands on her shoulders and pushing her back down. He'd been caring for her, and he was becoming familiar with her, more like an older brother than a vassal duke's son.

"Soon enough," he said. "I want to pack this so it will dry while we ride," he said. "If it rots we've wasted it, and that's disrespectful to Earth and Life."

Earth, the god they lived on and His daughter, Life, who was the mother of all living things upon Him. Lee never thought about which gods Hectaro prayed to – her father worshiped War and her mother Power, and nothing else ever crossed her mind.

She didn't want the poor antelope to have died for nothing, either.

"How long?"

"Give me an hour," he said. "You can saddle the horses if you're ready. Your fox has been standing watch for us and he does a good job. If someone comes by he'll let us know."

Lee felt concerned. "Have there been people?"

Hectaro shrugged. "A wagon the other day. A mounted patrol before nightfall. The volcano erupted last night and whoever survived is going to be coming this way, but we have time.

"There have been carrier birds flying all day, though," he added. "I'm more worried we're going to ride *into* someone looking to see what happened here."

Lee nodded. That wouldn't be good at all.

***

They packed the meat, they saddled the horses. They led their mounts outside and Hectaro used the pieces of the ruined table or counter from inside the cellar to cover the broken doors which they'd used to gain access here. Then he pushed dirt over the pieces and threw a few sods from the wagon tracks left by the travelers to cover those.

"No one should just pass by and see it," he said. "If someone is tracking us, they'll be distracted by it and waste time here looking for clues."

Lee nodded. She agreed.

They left the place at a trot. People who had once been ruled by the Cheyak, perhaps they themselves had built a home more than ten centuries ago, never knowing it would save the five of them today, two of the race of Men, two horses and a fox.

Who would use it next? What would they think, and when?

These thoughts filled Lee's head as she let the horses warm up, then pushed them to a canter. She pushed her sense of the Earth out before her, looking for any divot, ditch or trap that might impede their progress or hurt their horses. She found more and more evidence of tracks, all going to the west. Something like a watering hole was going to be there, she knew. The animals went there to drink, but didn't stay because it was too open and they needed to avoid predators.

And those predators were here. She needed to be wary but not worried – there would be easier game than they.

In an hour they could hear running water. In less than an hour after they found a river, running from the northwest to the southeast. Lee had seen this river – she knew it ran through Conflu for a long way.

She told Hectaro as much.

"The question, then," he said to her, "is, 'Do we follow it, or do we find a way to cross it, and if so, where?'"

Chapter Twenty-One

River Girl

Lee sat in the dark, the river churning before her, the night quiet except for the snorting of the horses behind her, and Hectaro's shuffling, holding their reins.

She unfocused her eyes. She fixed the image of hay in her mind – a pile of it, smelling fresh and dusty, soft in her fingers, mixed with stray leaves and foxtail.

She knew there would be hay in the loft in the stable, but of course she couldn't know how much or where. It changed every day. At this time of year it would rarely be used – more likely it would replace straw as bedding. This would be difficult enough to get her up out of her body again, and to make another trip across the land and down the river.

She called for the item – they could use the hay, regardless.

This time her being leapt up out of her body like an eagle from its perch. She could actually see Hectaro staring down at her, feel the fox curled up in her lap as she flew higher and higher, seeing more and more of the world around her.

The volcano she'd made erupt stood out like a beacon to her West, belching lava and ash. It had already flowed down to the walled city at its feet, destroying part of the wall on the mountain side. People were fleeing the city through the smoke and ash. The dead lined the streets and the area outside – both Confluni and their animals.

A wave of them were headed toward the river. More importantly, though, they'd gone to the northeast where the river flowed closer to the city, and they were already following it and, in some cases, travelling it in flat-bottomed boats.

She followed the waterway and found another walled city several days' travel down the river, and another afterward. The first city had an open river port – there would be no sailing discreetly past it. The river forked there, running to the southeast and the southwest.

The second city was farther up a tributary, another, mighty river flowing from the north to the south. There were more flat bottom boats on the river between the two of those.

The river could speed their travel if they could get past the cities, but it would be very dangerous to try it.

To the East, they would have to cross this river and another one and then enter a mighty forest, which covered daheeri before they could reach Tren Bay. She knew from her father those woods were heavily patrolled. He had travelled them with his Daff Kanaar allies and barely escaped with his life.

They'd *never* get through the Confluni forest. They needed to find a way down the river.

They needed a boat.

Thinking this distracted her, and Lee was caught completely unaware by a pile of hay as tall as a man and just as wide as it struck her body like catapult shot. The fox leapt away from her at the last minute and the horses reared. Lee was jarred back into her body, the hay stalks poking into her clothing and mixing into her unkempt hair.

She sighed, emerging from the pile as Hectaro struggled to get the horses back under control.

This could be the best thing to happen to her for a long time.

***

The river water ran cold and refreshing. Lee felt it wash the ash from her body and her hair – oh, her *hair*! This was the best it had felt since Galnesh Eldador.

Hectaro bathed next to her. He'd let her enter the water first – she'd already seen his naked body, not that it mattered. Her Andaron mother had always been rather frank about her body and raised her children the same, not prudish like Eldadorian nobles.

The horses had been unsaddled and hobbled. They'd washed the two equines down first in order that Lee and Hectaro not get dirty again.

The moon and stars in the night sky shown bright overhead. This would have been a wonderful experience if it weren't for the unimaginable danger they were in.

And, of course, for what they were trying to do.

"It's coming," Hectaro said, pointing up stream. Lee had already seen it – the flat-bottomed river boat with a lantern on its prow, gliding down the river with the current.

The boat maintained an arced canvas cover in the center, and one individual guided it. He stood next to the lantern with a pole in his hand, his eyes studying the water, looking out for rocks or debris that might damage their craft. People plied the river for all sorts of reasons – in Andoron and in Sental boats like this floated downstream and were dragged back up by teams of aurochs along cattle trails, long lines connecting the aurochs to the boats in the water. Lee had looked for signs of these trails here and not found them – either the trips tended to be one-way, they relied on sail power or they employed teams of strong men with poles to move the river boats back upstream. One might guess they moved the boats back up the river over land if one didn't know for certain the Confluni maintained no horses and their shaggy ponies wouldn't be up to the task.

Lee and Hectaro submerged themselves in the river until only the tops of their heads, their eyes and noses, were visible. Lee moved back toward the bank, Hectaro toward the middle of the river.

He'd left his sword with his horse but kept a dagger in each hand. He'd be fastening the remaining shards of her undergarments around his nether regions right now, more for protection than for modesty. Better not to expose an obvious vulnerability to an enemy.

The boat glided closer. Lee enhanced her vision. She didn't have the same senses in the water as she did on land, reaffirming her gifts came from the god Earth, not the sleeping goddess, Water.

The individual at the prow scanned the water. He was small, even for a Confluni. What fool left a child to tend the boat while the adults slept?

No, she realized, as the boat moved between them, and she readied her magic. *Not a child – another* Scitai! War's whiskers – was Conflu overrun with them?

The little man looked in her direction and then straightened. She remained perfectly still. He jabbed the river bottom with his pole, slowing the boat's progress, squinting out into the darkness.

Lee saw the brown hair and the clean shaven face by the lantern's light, then nothing as Hectaro pulled the little man backward over the boat's side.

Lee swam through the cool river to the boat's gunwale. The hull felt worn and slimy – it had been on the water for a long time, but usually more heavily loaded than it was now. She put her hands up on the boat's rising edge and pulled herself up to see into it, expecting anything.

She saw a collection of sleeping bags such as travelers preferred. She counted four, all occupied. Toward the back of the boat she could see wicker baskets covered in oiled leather to keep them safe from the water spray. She waited for movement and found none.

The Scitai's pole had been lost into the water, but these always had a spare. She pulled herself as quietly as she could into the boat, the cold air touching her naked body, seeing Hectaro on the other side. She slithered into the boat and, after a quick search, found a pole tied to the railing on the far side of the craft under the gunwale.

She pulled it loose and began poling the boat to the side of the river. Already they were downstream of the horses. Lee could see the fox waiting for them at the riverbank, unwilling to dampen its dainty paws.

The Scitai were stirring. Polling the river boat, changing its direction was hard work. The end of the boat had to be kept from swinging out wide, or the boat could go into a spin and she could then lose all control until it settled. With a little effort, they guided the river boat toward the shore, and were rewarded by the sound of its hull grinding on the river bottom as it found its way.

The gritty noise rousted the rest of the Scitai. No one who lived on a vessel like this didn't fear the night when they'd run adrift and have to fight to keep their livelihood.

Lee continued poling, beaching the craft, while Hectaro pulled himself up out of the water.

She didn't know what he'd had to do with the one who'd been guiding the craft, and so she couldn't guess the fate of these. She knew this was not palace intrigue which she could recover from if everything went wrong, however. The longer this went on, the closer they drew to their goal, the more she realized how serious their predicament was.

Chapter Twenty-Two

In the Guise of Another

While Lee made sure the river boat had been properly grounded, Hectaro roused the sleeping passengers at knife-point.

Lee had counted correctly – four Scitai: a plump female with long blonde hair, dressed in nothing but a linen sleeping-dress and three children, another female perhaps in her teens and two younger, a boy and a girl.

She saw no sign of the male who'd been poling the boat when they captured it.

The children huddled together. The female, clearly their mother, placed herself between the two groups, Scitai and Men. Lee used the pole as leverage and leapt naked from the boat to the river, planting the craft's end in the river shallows. She backed her way to the shore and their horses, keeping an eye on the boat, watching Hectaro argue by lamp light with the Scitai woman.

She tripped and landed on her butt. Something soft had been in her path. She reached down to her feet and found the body of the missing Scitai, face down in the water where the river current had dragged it.

She pushed her feet underneath her and squatted by the Scitai male, flipped him over and saw where Hectaro had opened up his throat. At the time it had been a good plan – they couldn't know what they'd find onboard or who they'd have to fight.

In their current predicament this would likely work against them.

They'd planned to take hostages and to use them to pole the boat past the city downstream. That wouldn't likely be happening now. At the same time, they'd have to decide if they could afford to leave these Scitai behind. The Scitai they'd encountered here seemed to be loyal to Conflu and had no stake in helping them – the more evidence they left of their passing, the more they assured the Confluni government would come looking for them before they could escape.

Lee stood and checked on Hectaro. He had the Scitai sitting in a row in the front of the boat and was binding their hands behind them. The children were all crying and the woman, probably their mother, was trying to be strong.

She turned on her heel and ran back to the horses and to her clothes. The fox appeared out of the darkness and followed her, nipping at her heels as she moved. She smiled despite herself. Finding her clothes and stepping into her pants while the fox danced around her, she sent her senses out one more time through the Earth, to feel out what might be going on around them in the dark.

A few stray animals drinking at the water's edge. Nothing walking on two legs for as far as she could sense. Of course the river remained a blank to her – she couldn't get a feel for what might be in it, and the night ran too dark for her to see for herself.

She couldn't imagine how this was going to go well.

***

Lee returned with the horses, the fox and their supplies, already packed. The riverboat seemed large enough to carry both horses if the two of them didn't move around too much, and the covered portion was barely large enough to cover them. Getting the horses actually into the boat might prove difficult – there was no ramp so they'd need to step over the side, but they'd need to not ground the boat with the horses' weight and make it impossible to move back out to the river. The process would definitely take some effort.

"Where's my husband?" the Scitai woman was demanding. "Where's Gered?"

Hectaro just ignored her. "Are they ready?"

"I don't see how we'll get them onboard," Lee answered him. "This has no ramp, and if we leave it here and pull them in then we won't be able to push off. If we move it farther out, I doubt they'll be able to get in without tipping it."

Hectaro frowned. Clearly he'd been counting on a ramp. "Can't you…" he said, and then waved a hand in the air.

She smiled. "It doesn't work that way," she told him. "I know how to do useful things like you've seen, but I can't move horses around through the air."

"You can move the Earth, though, can't you?" Hectaro asked.

"I can do that," she agreed.

"So we can load the horses here," Hectaro said, "and you can move the earth underneath the boat and make a channel…"

"And we can get out through there," she said. "Yes – yes, I think I can do that."

They pushed the Scitai's possessions out from under the canopy. The sleeping bags, some pillows and a bag of clothing, a few wooden toys for the children – the Scitai watched as what little they had was taken by someone stronger. The Scitai woman alternated between watching them and turning her head around, probably expecting her dead husband to come rescue them.

Lee felt the weight of their situation on her soul. Yes, they had to survive. But the price of their survival was climbing.

Did being a Mordetur make other lives less valuable than hers?

"Alright, let's load them," Hectaro said, once he'd cleared a space. He stepped off of the boat and into the river, taking Bastard by the reins. They didn't really have lead ropes for them and the reins gave them the control they needed.

Bastard didn't want to know anything about stepping up into the boat. They tried Singer but she was clearly set off by Bastard. They tried taking a running start, then they tried just leaning back on the reins and keeping tension, and waiting.

"Blindfold them," the Scitai female told them. Both Lee and Hectaro turned to where the Scitai knelt next to her children.

"You cover their heads," she said. "They can't see so they're less afraid."

Lee and Hectaro looked at each other. Lee shrugged. "Try it," she said.

Hectaro took his tunic from their supplies and threw it over Bastard's head. The stallion tried to shake it off, tried to step back away from them, then settled.

Hectaro pulled him toward the boat, then when he was close picked up his left front hoof and placed it in the boat. He waited, then did the same with the right, and pulled on the reins.

The stallion trotted right in, banging his hooves on the railing. He pranced a good bit but then settled, and Hectaro pulled him under the canopy.

Once he was in, Singer followed right along, wanting to be with him.

The Scitai woman allowed herself a self-satisfied grin. Hectaro reached for his tunic.

"No!" Lee and the Scitai woman said at the same time. Hectaro pulled his hand away.

"If you hood him, you leave him hooded," Lee said. "Let him see he's where he didn't want to be now and he'll kick hell out of everything around him to get out." The Scitai woman nodded.

"So what will he do when the boat starts moving?" Hectaro asked them.

The Scitai woman shrugged. "You can always take the blindfold off if you think you need to," she said. "Try putting it back on, though, once it's off."

This time Lee nodded.

The fox leapt on board the boat. He sniffed the Scitai, then their possessions, then ran to the back of the boat and curled up by their supplies, pressing his side against the wicker basket.

Hectaro leapt off of the boat in the meantime, donned his clothes with the exception of his boots, and then threw those and their provisions in the stern with their possessions.

Lee leapt off after him when he was done and put her head close to his.

"What about them?" she asked.

"What *about* them?" he responded.

"Do we bring them?"

Hectaro pulled his head back and frowned. "How can we?" he asked her. "They'll want to know where the father is, and then they'll want vengeance. We'll never be able to trust them and what do we have to hold over them? I doubt the woman can guide the boat on her own."

Lee looked back at the Scitai, all watching the fox, then back at Hectaro. "We *can't* kill them," she said. "Not after they…"

"After they *what*?" Hectaro hissed. "Helped us? The woman's trying to make happen exactly what you're feeling. She'll get your sympathy to stay alive, and then run as fast as her legs will carry her to the first Confluni guardsman she can find."

"I don't think…" Lee began.

"I killed her *husband*," Hectaro said, a little louder, and put his hand on her shoulder. "When they figure out what I did, all they'll want is to hurt us."

"They're days from any help," Lee said.

"Do you want pursuit days behind us?" Hectaro asked her.

Lee sighed. Hectaro stepped up into the boat, a dagger in his hand behind him and, without looking at the Scitai, stepped up behind them.

The woman wasn't fooled.

"The children – " she began.

Hectaro took the youngest girl by the hair on the back of her head, pulled her head back to expose her throat and slashed it. The girl tried to gasp and struggle, but her own blood choked her.

The other children weren't quite aware yet of what was going on.

"No!" the Scitai woman screamed.

The two remaining children turned their heads to her, and Hectaro took the only boy by the back of the head. Lee forced herself not to look away as Hectaro dispatched him.

The youngest daughter fell forward. The older daughter noticed her and tried to throw herself forward.

"Vera!" she screamed. Hectaro had to reach for her. She squirmed on the floor, fighting for her life. Hectaro finally took her by her collar and pulled her back up to her knees.

"No!" the mother screamed. "No! Leave one! Leave one!"

The eldest daughter screamed again and tried to pull away. Hectaro reached around her with the knife and pulled the blade across her throat, making a bad job of it.

The boy fell forward.

"You bastard!" the woman screamed at him. "I curse you! In the name of Eveave, the All-Mother, I curse you. What you've taken will be taken from you a thousand times!"

She didn't resist as Hectaro took her by the hair. Trying to look back into his face, she hissed, "I curse you!"

Hectaro cut her throat. He pitched the bodies up onto the riverbank, and then found the father's body and laid it across the rest.

"When you move the earth," he said, "try to cover them."

"It will work better if I'm on land, I think," Lee said, feeling numb, as if he'd killed a part of her with the Scitai family.

He nodded and hopped back into the riverboat. The horses hadn't reacted much to the screaming or the smell of blood. Bastard had been trained as a war horse and that sort of thing didn't bother him. Singer had seen her share of violence in the last year.

Lee unfocused her eyes, then saw the mud and gravel underneath the riverboat with her mind. She willed it to slide out from under the boat and onto the bank, over the Scitai family, so tiny, none of them over three feet tall, the little ones barely one foot.

She kept drawing the mud and gravel out, more and more, covering them, covering the area near them. Still the boat didn't move. She pulled more from downstream of the boat, hoping the water filling this new empty area would dislodge the boat.

"Maybe this boat is too small," Hectaro said.

Lee didn't know if she could bear it, if this were all done for nothing.

She pulled out a huge swath of mud and the riverboat swung free, catching Hectaro by surprise. The horses stomped nervously as he dug in with the pole, trying to keep the riverboat steady.

It sank down to within a hand's breadth of the gunwales but didn't sink. Lee charged out to the boat's side, stepping up onto the mound she'd built over the Scitai family, and leapt for the boat. Hectaro caught her in one arm and brought the pole around behind her, striking her smartly in the back of the head. Lee saw stars but didn't lose consciousness. She felt the bump on the back of her head but didn't bleed.

The riverboat picked up pace and slid out to the middle of the river. Hectaro poked the bottom of the river with his pole to guide it, making it float true.

As the sun rose to the east, Lee saw the fox in the front of the boat, licking the blood on the deck.

Tears shown wet on Lee's cheeks, mourning the death both of an innocent family and her childhood, both long before their time.

Chapter Twenty-Three

Jeng Chao

For four days and nights, the river boat slid down the Jeng-Jeng River toward the city of Jeng Chao, from the city of Shin Dae, which they'd probably destroyed. Even from this distance they could see the ash the volcano was throwing into the sky.

They knew this because the Scitai man, Gered, had kept a journal of his travels, and they'd found and read it. Gered had travelled back and forth up and down the Jeng-Jeng River for years, met his wife here, birthed his children here. They'd hoped to start a trade route, moving the crops from Shin Dae to Jeng Chao, and then moving back the goods produced in Jeng Chao to Shin Dae and the city across the mountains, Jeng Shin.

Scitai in Conflu were much like Scitai on the Silent Isle under the Trenboni. They were considered second class citizens and they earned their way despite the people who ruled them. The Confluni called them 'honored brothers,' but treated them more like vassals.

One passage stuck in Lee's mind, and she remembered it over and over:

The Scitai nation actually pre-dates the Confluni, who really didn't come to power until after the fall of the Cheyak. The Scitai were allies to the Cheyak and worshipped Eveave, the Taker and the Giver, as we do today. Because Men breed more rapidly, even though they live little more than half as long as a Scitai, and because they think nothing of raping the land and taking from it what they want, they multiply like ants when good people spread their common food on the ground to share.

You can't overcome Men, you move along with them, and you wait. Eventually the Scitai nation will rise again, and Men will build it.

The person who wrote this, Lee felt, was no uneducated riverman. This was a person who thought deep thoughts and, more importantly, recorded them so he or someone else could reflect on them later. Gered worked with his hands but thought like a scholar – so different from the comical image her people maintained of the tiny Scitai.

Lee needed to speak to Karel of Stone when she saw him again – her father's Scitai friend and Daff Kanaar ally.

Their days on the river passed simply: one guided the boat while the other slept. Whoever was awake fed the horses two times a day and cleaned up after them about ten times a day. The fox usually lay on Lee or close by her. The river ran swift and they could cover more than 100 daheeri in a day.

They would read the journal, or they would talk about what they read. They discussed in depth what they might do to get past Jeng Chao, and no plan seemed like it would work.

On their fourth day Lee woke Hectar with the news they'd been expecting for two days:

"There are other people on the river," she informed him.

***

They could see the other boat, almost exactly like their own, approaching them. Three big Men were poling it against the current. Why they'd try to do that escaped Lee – it would be easier to put the boat on a cart and pull it on the land, even if they pulled it themselves. No matter, they would have to pass this craft in less than an hour, and neither of them looked even remotely Confluni.

They'd looked for some hint in the journal telling them the Confluni kept slaves from the rest of Fovea, but nothing. All of the people in Conflu were Men or Scitai.

"A glamour?" Hectaro asked her.

A glamour would allow her to look like another being. She'd seen her share of Confluni. She could look like one if she wanted to.

She'd never really studied glamour. She knew the principles but not the practice.

They had nothing else.

"I'll try," she promised him.

Hectaro hung one of their leather skins on one end of the boat's canopy, and another skin on the other. Either one only really covered the upper third of the opening's height, but people usually didn't look past things like that unless they had a reason.

He'd lay down with the horses and wait with his sword. If things got bad or the glamour failed, then he'd be their second line of defense.

Neither of them could know how long the glamour would last or how effectively he could defend them. River workers were a beefy lot and fought more frequently than regular farmers or villagers. Without a group of natives to guide them, however, this was likely the best they could hope for.

In the back of her mind, Lee wondered if she didn't actually deserve to fail.

"Ok, we'd better start," Hectaro informed her.

There were Confluni in her father's Wolf Soldier guard. This sort of thing was easier with a real pattern to follow, and Lee picked the form of a stout fellow she'd met named Tran Li. He kept his hair longer than most Confluni, but she altered it to be average. He was muscular and squat, with a square jaw and beetle brow. His high cheekbones topped drawn cheeks and his legs were a little bowed – Lee had never learned why. She unfocused her eyes and took Tran's image into her head, and then she imagined a large bucket floating over her head, suspended from nothing, filled with clay and dyed.

She spilled the bucket and she felt the contents wash over her, surprisingly warm, covering her, filling in the gaps in her body where Tran was different from her. In her mind she felt the change as it took place, guided it, felt the transition from Lee to Tran Li.

Hectaro watched her, his jaw open, forcing himself to verify their surroundings once as the transition took place and Lee changed.

It took almost a minute, but finally Lee felt like she'd become Tran.

"How do I look?" she asked Hectaro.

"You look like a Confluni man," he said. "That's the strangest thing I've ever seen, Lee. You seemed to flow from your head to shoulders – I can't really describe it except to say that if I could see a figurine being dipped in wax from inside the pot, that would have been you."

Lee really didn't know how to respond to Hectaro so she just nodded. She looked around her on the river.

They were fast-gaining on the boat polling toward them. She leaned on her own river pole and pushed the boat away from the center, making way for them.

Their behavior might be considered anti-social. These people might normally approach each other and talk and gossip, but if that were true they were doomed anyway. If her accent didn't give her away, the contents of her boat would.

It suddenly seemed strange to her that the Scitai family had been travelling down the river with an empty boat. They could have been porting refugees if they had no wares. She and Hectaro should have found something, legal or otherwise, in the boat, but they'd covered every inch of it in their boredom and found nothing.

The fox leaped to the side of the boat and put its forepaws on the gunwales, staring at the other boat as they passed it. One of the four males poling the boat saw him and pointed, and the rest of them looked. She waved a hand and smiled as they passed, all four of them did the same, then went back to their poling before they could lose their pace. They followed a pattern of the two in back pushing, then the two in front as the ones in back repositioned their poles. In this way they traveled up the river like a horse in a slow-motion gallop.

She watched them for a while as she passed, then turned her attention back to the river, guiding the boat back to the center and pushing against an under-water rock as they came too near it. In less than ten minutes they were over a daheer past the four men and their boat.

She looked to the east again and saw another boat. She waited and could see they were gaining on it. Another group was poling their way up the river, and so it made sense for her to keep up the glamour.

She sighed. This might turn out to be a long day.

They travelled for two more hours, passing other river boats one or two at a time, never coming near them, never doing more than waving.

A few noticed the fox, most seemed too busy to care. Polling up a river was hard work and the river men had little extra energy to spare.

Then they sighted the city of Jeng Chao.

Another huge, walled city, with a bustling port rose up to their southeast, guardsmen walking along the parapets evident by the sun shining down on their steel, crops outside the walls growing out for more than a daheer in every direction. Lee saw a dozen wind mills at the water's edge pumping water into irrigation ditches for fields, and yoked aurochs dragging plows and wagons all around the fields. The month was either late in Chaos or early in Water, and either was awfully late in the season for sowing seeds, or early for harvesting.

The glamour was starting to weigh on her. Her body was smaller than Tran Li's and she didn't see out through his eyes or move her arms from his shoulders, so when she poled the river boat she had a weird illusion from her perspective of the pole floating around in front of her as the magic matched the poles movement to the glamour. She had a double-vision aspect to everything she saw, and it had started giving her a headache.

They gained rapidly on the city, the smells of human and animal waste flowing over them as the wind changed direction and blew down the river. Rotting food, smoke from furnaces and fires, the reek of human sweat and the earthy smell of fresh-tilled soil reminded her of a ship pulling into Galnesh Eldador, even though the Eldadorian capitol didn't actually have much tilled land around it. Where the Confluni sat right on top of their farms, the Eldadorians would build on land unfit for farming and then walk to their fields.

"What's the traffic like?" Hectaro asked her.

"The traffic?" she responded. Even his voice irritated her for some reason. She knew the constant effort was making her testy. She'd gone to the back of the boat twice for food and water to sustain her and was about to go again.

"Boats moving in and out of the city through the port," he said, and to her he sounded like he was talking to a child. "Do all of the river boats go into the city, do some pass by?"

Lee watched. There were boats poling out of the city and toward them, and there were others from farther down the river which seemed to be about to pass the city by, while others poled their way in. She didn't see a single sailed ship, neither did she see one pulled by aurochs.

There were no boats behind them and none ahead. She couldn't tell what river boats from their direction did.

"I can't tell," she said. "There's only about a score of boats and they're all over the place. Most go in the city but not all of them, and we're the only ones coming down the river."

"War's Whiskers," Hectaro swore. Lee bridled. This wasn't her fault.

"I think we have to try to go past the city," he said. The sun was high in the sky. If they passed the city then they'd do it over the next two hours with plenty of daylight left in the day.

If someone in the city wanted to give chase, they'd have an easy time of it, and then they'd either lose the river for traveling or be running their entire time on it.

They'd left all of their easy answers on the other side of the volcano, it seemed, and even then those answers hadn't seemed very easy.

Chapter Twenty-Four

What Happened on the River

Just before they achieved the city of Jeng Chao, another river branched from the Jeng-Jeng and ran back to the West. Lee would have thought the way the rivers met impossible had she not seen it. There had to be some giant rocky base or something similar to keep the jutting peninsula that held the water from the source of the mighty river from eroding a more natural break, however Lee couldn't see it and it looked just like the rest of the river to her.

She really had to bear down to pole past it, and ended up moving the river boat more toward the north bank of the river. The current was exceptionally strong, and of course Hectaro couldn't stand up and help her.

She saw at least a dozen boats bobbing down the river, most of them from the Jeng-Jeng. Others of them were moored off of the shore. She had to cross in front of one of the boats polling west to get out of the current, and she could hear the four men who had to halt their progress cursing her in Confluni as they passed.

"What's going on?" Hectaro insisted, worry in his voice.

"The current is strong and I'm not," she said through grit teeth. They were directly to the north of the city now and the smells were overwhelming. "We're getting in other peoples' way trying to get out of the current and they're getting mad."

"What can I do?" Hectaro pressed her.

She sighed. Typical male, she thought. He didn't like being helpless and he couldn't accept the idea she had nothing for him to do. If he stood up they might turn out half the city, and if he didn't and she crashed her boat into someone else's, they might be in even worse straights.

She bore down on the pole and dug in to the earth bottom. The pole slipped, caught and slipped again.

Another boat encroached on their space, meeting them head-to-head. She wanted to pass to the north of them, however they seemed to want to do the same thing.

She decided it would be better to let them have the right of way and let the current move her to their south. They passed close enough where she could have leapt onto their deck from hers if she wanted. She'd have been more gratified if she could have ordered Hectaro to do it with his sword drawn.

The thought gave her a smile, and one of the men on the other boat caught it. He must have thought she was doing this on purpose, but for whatever reason he shouted at her in rapid-fire Confluni, Lee translating a few words she didn't think were at all complimentary, and then as she passed one of their poles found the aft quarter of their gunwales.

They sent the boat in a spin. Already over-loaded, they pitched sickeningly to one side as Lee braced her feet and tried to right the boat with her one pole.

The pole snapped. They'd made another but she'd spend precious minutes unbundling it from where they'd tied it to the rail.

Bastard neighed, Singer neighed after him, and then they bumped into each other. The stallion's motion rocked the boat and then he kicked out in fear and anger, falling as he did so.

There was nothing for it now. Hectaro was up and trying to get the stallion under control. The fox ran back and forth across the forward part of the boat. Lee ran for Singer, taking her by the make-shift leather halter she'd made for her two days before.

***

The mare kicked out, catching the stallion as he tried to rise. A dozen people on three boats near them, four of them on the boat they'd just passed, started shouting and pointing.

So, of course, her concentration broke, and suddenly she was a brown-haired Eldadorian girl with a horse whose like was not seen on Confluni soil.

The boat they'd passed started trying to turn itself around, the men onboard digging their poles into the river bottom.

It was too much. Lee was frustrated and she'd been expending her magic like she'd been expending her breath. She'd killed innocents, she'd abandoned allies, she'd birthed a volcano which had probably already killed thousands.

No, she thought. Not anymore.

She unfocused her eyes, and she called on power she had no business wielding.

Planks shattered in boats all around her. The broken pole in her hand flew like a falcon into the breast of the man who'd pushed their boat with her pole. He dropped the implement and clutched at the foreign object protruding from his rib cage, then fell forward into the river, over the side of his own boat as his shipmates reached for him.

They joined him a moment later as their boat sank beneath the waves.

Other sailors, their boats vanishing into the river beneath their feet, swam for their gunwales. Lee crossed the boat and took Bastard's halter from Hectaro while the stallion struggled to his feet. Next to him Singer was pawing the deck beneath her.

"Repel them," she ordered him, pushing him away.

"What – Lee, what did you? What are we?" he stammered.

"Just pick up your sword and kill anyone who comes near us," she said. She put a tiny hand on the bridge of the great stallion's nose, as she'd seen her father do with his own horse, Blizzard. "Just do it."

He picked up his sword off of the deck. One of the horses had stepped on it and bent the point. He ran to the gunwales to port, and then to starboard, judging their distance from the rivermen who were swimming toward them.

Lee couldn't be bothered with the rivermen. She focused on the stallion. She had no magic for this, but she'd been raised by a woman who knew horses. She'd been around them her whole life.

Singer dragged the decking with her iron shoes, raising a few splinters. Lee back-handed her across her soft nose.

"Stop that," she warned the mare. The stallion shied again but she pulled its head down toward hers, rubbing it on the flat spot between its eyes, cooing to him, feeling calm in a sea of turmoil to make him calm.

Bastard could sink them without even trying, and then they'd be done in. She could see past the stallion to the river banks where Confluni were collecting. The river stretched over a daheer wide, or they'd be throwing things or firing arrows at them.

They still might.

Confluni screamed as Hectaro struck them with his sword. It wasn't long before a hand landed still-twitching on the deck past the horses. The fox ran to it, picked it up in its needle-sharp teeth and ran for the wicker basket where it could devour the prize.

The horses were settling in the chaos around them. Hectaro pushed past her to verify no one swam up behind them. Lee heard another scream, and then a gurgle.

They glided past the port. Within its river wharf, Lee could see Confluni with weapons and reddish-brown leather armor, scrambling for more of the river boats.

This might have been worse, Lee thought, but that didn't mean it wasn't very, very bad.

***

They passed the city. Lee sank another river boat as it tried to pole itself into their way. The wooden craft were of the earth, and thus answered to her power.

She didn't need to make the boards explode. Doing so had been a measure of her frustration. When she focused, she could just move a board out of alignment and send the boat to the bottom of the river.

When the boats sank they left the rivermen behind. They could swim after them and try to scramble over their gunwales, or they could swim to shore. Some had made it there and were trying to follow them.

A running man could easily keep up with a riverboat, however there were obstacles on the riverbanks to be avoided, and a running man would tire. The river never did. Pursuers might last even an hour, but then fell off. Eventually they'd come up on someone with one of their shaggy ponies and then they would have a permanent shadow. Already there were half a dozen boats far enough behind them where they could see them, but out of range of her magic. It wasn't like they were going to suddenly find another river. In a chase like this there was no evading the enemy.

They'd been found. Now it was a matter of time. Two flights of messenger pigeons had already flown overhead and Lee had knocked them out of the sky, putting them to sleep in mid-flight. She was using too much magic and she felt exhausted.

"Sleep," Hectaro told her.

"What?" she couldn't believe this. What was he *thinking*? This was the height of pursuit.

"Sleep," he said again. "I can see how tired you are. We'll need your power, you need your rest. Eat and then sleep while they're still afraid of you. They're going to start thinking of something else to try soon enough – when that comes I'll wake you if you're not awake already. You'll want your strength when it happens."

She hated it but she had to agree. Right now the Confluni's collective hand had been smacked, and it was smarting. The pain would wear off. New persons who hadn't seen what she had done would join the chase, and they'd test her, not believing what she might be capable of.

They might be preparing an ambush in front of them for all she knew, as well.

She sat and the fox leapt up into her lap, its gruesome prize half-gnawed in its mouth. Lee took it and threw it over the side. The fox meant to leap over the gunwales for it but she restrained it and fed it jerked meat to distract it. She fed herself, watching Hectaro who, in turn, watched the boats behind them, the people at the riverbanks, and scanned the river before them for enemies.

He's not a coward, she informed herself. She'd misjudged this man. Hectaro had called on courage when another might have surrendered to the inevitability of their situation. He'd been strong and done the brutal things, stood the long watches, and carried the extra burden needed to keep them both alive.

Thinking what a great team the two of them made, Lee drifted off into a dreamless sleep, under a warm sun and a cloudless blue sky.

Chapter Twenty-Five

Race to the Border

A cool wind blew across Lee's face. She burst awake all-of-a-sudden, seeing nothing but the dark, hearing nothing but the water lapping at the river boat's sides, smelling the horses and their manure, feeling the fox's luxurious fur as it lay curled in her lap.

She'd slept sitting up. Her face burned where the sun had touched it. The sun beat them mercilessly on the river, but the glamour had offered her some protection.

An Andaron after her mother, her skin tended to brown, not burn. She knew her father would be peeling like an onion after the first sunny day in Earth's month.

She waited, calling her magic, enhancing her sight. The moon was out but the horses were just blobs until she focused her power.

She couldn't make out Hectaro anywhere. She could see the river water on either side. He might have fallen overboard or, more likely, someone might have swum up on them and Hectaro might have been pulled over the side, protecting her.

An attack would have upset the horses and the fox. No, she thought. Something else must have happened.

"Hectaro?" she whispered.

"Here," she heard behind her.

She leapt to her feet, the horses snorting, the fox dashing to the front of the boat and curling up defensively at the prow. She turned and there he was, two horse blankets underneath him, his sword at his side, stretched out behind the chest she'd been leaning against.

"Were you sleeping?" she asked. Both of them sleeping would be a bad idea – someone needed to keep the watch in such a dangerous predicament.

"Not really, no," she said. "Your father taught the first Wolf Soldiers how to have what he called "waking dreams," letting the mind wander while a part remains aware. This has been passed on and improved on in the Pack ever since. That's how I've been able to take so many watches. You stay sort of awake while sort of sleeping. It isn't as good as sleep but you can go for days."

"What's been happening?" Lee pressed him. She didn't know Wolf Soldiers did this and it sort of bothered her that her father hadn't shared this with her.

Her mother spoke often of the special relationship her father had with his Wolf Soldiers, and it often reminded her he had no such relationship with his children. At least – not his daughters.

Thoughts of her father's children brought up thoughts of Chawnee, and it occurred to her she hadn't thought about her baby sister in a long, long time.

"Well, they tried to pole up on us a little after you went to sleep," he said. "But all I did was push us just as fast. That went on for more than an hour before they gave up. When I settled down, they waited a while and they tried it again."

"And now?"

"And now," he said, "they are hanging back – probably sleeping while the sun is down. You can see their boat lanterns."

Lee ran to the back of the boat and saw the boat lanterns hanging from the prows of their river craft, lighting the way for them and clearly marking where they were, more than two daheeri down the river by her best estimate.

"Why would they do that?" she asked him.

"Do what?" he countered.

She turned, leaving a foot on the gunwale.

"Why would they mark themselves so clearly," she asked him, watching him sit up on the horse blankets. "The moon is out – they don't need the light. Why aren't they trying to move dark and overtake us when it's hard for us to see them?"

Hectaro might have answered, but she didn't hear it, because a hand as strong as steel took her by the ankle and pulled her over the gunwale and into the river.

***

Panic.

Suffocation.

Her first instinct had been to take a deep breath, and doing so had filled her lungs with water. Someone strong was swimming away from the river's surface and dragging her, and she couldn't do anything but clutch at the water and gag.

She couldn't focus her mind for spell casting, she couldn't do anything. Little white lights flashed before her eyes. She'd been caught entirely unaware, and if this person wanted to kill her then all they had to do was wait.

Something jarred the water to one side of her, and the hand released her ankle. She kicked her feet, she clutched with her hands, and she tried to reach the surface.

Pain! Her lungs and her nasal passages burned for the water in them.

No. She focused. She could swim to the bottom as easily as the top. She needed to be still, and wait, and let her own buoyancy take her to the top.

So hard. So painful. Her lungs burned, her brain told her '*Breathe!*' and her body had to fight it. She spread her arms out, then her legs, and looked where she thought 'up' might be, searching for the water's surface. She turned and, finally, she saw the moon.

Three hard kicks and she broke the surface. Her face found the cold night air and she puked up water. She sank and then had to kick to put her face above the water again. This time she got a strangled gasp of air, cold and painful in her lungs.

A wooden hull emerged from the night. Dark blobs moved on top of it. She didn't need to enhance her vision to know what was going on.

They'd set the lamps on the some of the ships, and probably on the prow and stern of one in order to look like two, and then another had poled up after them. When they'd come close then one of them had slipped into the river to overtake them in the dark, and then likely waited for someone to do what she had done.

This Confluni boat was overtaking her now, probably heading for their own boat. Once these people controlled their horses, their own capture became inevitable.

Someone broke the surface a few yards away from her, and someone else afterward. She heard the 'thunk' of flesh striking flesh, then heard it again, followed by splashing.

Hectaro was fighting whomever had pulled her overboard.

She focused her will, reached out with her mind, and sank the boat with the people on it, warping the boards in its bottom. They'd moved as many fighters as they could into as few boats as they dared, and left the boats overloaded. The boat was doomed before the swearing could begin.

The Confluni started shouting in their native language. Others answered from the water, near her. She heard flesh strike flesh again, near her, almost where she could reach it. In a fight man-to-man, she'd expect Hectaro to prevail against a Confluni, but Water was an equalizer.

If they wanted to prevail, she had to unbalance the scales again.

"Hectaro!" she called out.

"Here!" he answered. She enhanced her sight. She saw him, face-to-face with two Confluni, another closing in behind him. Their weight would have him under water in a moment.

She reached for him with her mind, to the earthy parts of him, his flesh and his clothing. She turned her mind down the river and she found their boat, the horses stomping, the fox running between the gunwales, a Confluni with a spear standing with his foot on the stern, squinting for them into the night.

She drew the boat as well, as sharply as she could. The Confluni fell back into the middle and the fox struck, teeth and claws reaching for vulnerable eyes. Hectaro flew through the water to her, she to him and both for the boat.

The Confluni came swimming after, but now they had no boat and their own allies were screaming for them. In the center of a swift river at night a person could die feet from the shore and never know it, just slip exhausted beneath the surface of the water.

"Hey! Hey! Hey!" Hectaro exclaimed, not knowing what she was doing or, most likely, even if it were her doing it.

In a moment she had her hand on the gunwale, and a moment later he had his hand on her. From the boat they heard the fox's hiss and the screams of the Confluni man he'd attacked.

She helped push Hectaro up over the gunwale, then she waited. She heard the scuffle and felt the boat rock. The horses were becoming more agitated and the stallion might decide to react at any moment. Still hooded, if either horse broke the boat or fell out of it, then both were doomed and either Lee and Hectaro or the Confluni would be hard-pressed to save them.

The Confluni flew over her head into the river. Hectaro's hand reached over the stern and took a fist full of her shirt and a good portion of her hair, and yanked her up into the safety of their boat.

He turned to the horses and she rose up next to him. The fox was sitting in the prow licking blood from its claws. Bastard was bobbing his head and stomping, Singer next to him. They'd already damaged the deck of their boat, and there was water beading up by the splinters they'd created.

She extended her will and tried to re-knit the boards. Unfortunately, she was exhausted and she didn't know very much about this. The wood expanded like so many straws and water began seeping in through it.

"Oh, no!" Hectaro said, noting it. She shook her head. She tried to use her power to repair what she'd done, but she clearly made it worse.

She just didn't know how to do this, no matter how much power she had.

"For the shore!" Hectaro told her. He took both horses by their hoods. "Get the pole!"

"They'll catch us!" she protested.

"We'll die in the river," he answered. She had to admit, he was right. When the horses felt the water on their fetlocks, they were going to react and nothing was going to stop them.

She grabbed up the pole and she pushed toward the western shore. They would be near another of the Confluni cities, she knew. On the eastern side of the river they were closer to home and closer to danger at the same time.

She couldn't be sure *what* she'd run into now.

The water lapped around her ankles. She tried to reach out for the Eastern shore with her power but she had little left. The pole in her hands crunched into pebbles and river silt in the riverbed as she pushed the sinking boat toward the shore. She could feel the vibration in her hands.

The breeze from the shore pulled her hair, bringing with it the smells of jasmine and overturned dirt. She felt its cool touch on her wet skin. The fox raised its head, its eyes searching to their west, telling her they must be closing on land.

Lee wanted to tell Hectaro, but as she turned she saw him with his hands on his stallion's head, trying to calm him. Singer had pressed her side to the larger horse's rib cage. If Hectaro could calm the male, Singer would likely follow his lead.

Lee jabbed the poled into the riverbed again, and it stopped short far sooner than she'd expected. She took a new grip on the pole and the boat swung sharply to one side.

The deck shifted, the horses snorted. The fox leapt from the gunwale to the west, and Lee struggled to get the pole back against the river bottom.

When she did, it touched silt even sooner than before. The boat spun around on this new axis and the pole turned in her hands.

One of the horses neighed, then the other. Hecataro hissed at her but she couldn't pay attention. It took her all of her strength to urge the boat back to the west.

When she did, she felt the deck crunch the shore. The shock of landing pushed the horses farther than they were willing to go. Bastard reared a third of his height and called out his challenge. When his hooves touched the deck, the boards shattered.

Hectaro ripped the cover from the horse's eyes, then did the same for Singer. Bastard gathered himself and leapt from the sinking boat. The mare followed him.

Hectaro spared a single look for Lee then put his foot on the gunwale. The boat, now without the additional weight of the horses, lurched to one side and Lee found herself leaning on the pole in her hands just to keep her feet. Hectaro tried to leap from the boat but, over-balanced, fell head-first into the water. When the boat rocked back Lee fell into the bottom of it, the water covering her legs.

Someone shouted in Confluni to their west. Hectaro called out, "Run!" and then she heard no more from him.

Chapter Twenty-Six

Out of the Frying Pan

Lee stood in the boat just in time to see stocky, yellow-skinned Confluni warriors in leather armor and pointed steel caps take the port side of her boat in their strong hands and start pulling it to shore.

She raised a hand white with power and held it out toward them. It was about as much as she could do with what remained of her power, but they wouldn't know the truth.

Predictably, the warriors gasped and retreated. The boat started to move back out into the current. If she let that happen, she'd be swimming with no horses, no fox and no Hectaro.

She stood and an arrow planted itself in the deck beside her. Another followed on her other side. She knew what the arrows meant – they had archers, they had their night vision, they knew where she was.

She raised her hands, palms out, above her head, and let the white light die. The Confluni were back at the gunwales and they pulled the sinking boat to shore.

Rough hands pulled her from the boat to dry land. Someone
sparked a torch in the darkness and she saw men holding their horses,
others on either side of Hectaro who, on his knees, had his hands tied
behind his back and blood oozing from the corner of his mouth, and no
sign of her fox.

A warrior in more intricate armor, with wide, scalloped shoulder
guards and a short black cape hanging behind him, snarled something
to her in Confluni, but she shook her head. He slapped her and
repeated himself, but she shook her head again.

As a part of her studies her mentors had tried to teach her this
difficult language but she'd resisted it. What was the point, when she
could just ask her father?

She wouldn't mind seeing the Emperor here now.

"What you here?" the warrior demanded in the language common
to Men. It was said once, when the Cheyak had ruled Fovea, all Men
had been of one race and spoke one language. Based on how different
they all were now, she'd always found a universal language very hard
to believe.

"We are lost," she said. "Powerful magic – we just want to go
home."

The man slapped her again. Hectaro shouted at him but one of the
warriors guarding him just slapped him on the back of his head.
Hectaro turned his face to the man, his eyes filled with hatred, and the
Confluni warrior raised his hand again.

"Enough!" someone shouted from outside of the torch's circle of
light. A woman's voice; the warriors stood back and lowered their
faces. From farther east a Confluni woman and ten more warriors
stepped out of the gloom.

She was slight, with long black hair, wearing a thick, glossy red
silk dress and open-toed sandals. She kept her chin raised, clearly used
to looking down at the rest of the world, even though she stood a few
inches shorter than the Eldadorian Princess.

Lee knew this woman – she was called 'Jing Wei.' Her father was
the Confluni Emperor. When Lee's father had become a King, she'd
been one of his suitors, come to forge an alliance with the Eldadorian
nation in its new-found growth.

Instead, Rancor Mordetur had married Shela, a slave. The shame
for the Confluni princess had been unbearable and she'd spent years in
a convent. When the Confluni Emperor's wives could give him no

male children, she'd returned to the Imperial palace as the next in line and been forced to marry the son of a military family.

Lee knew all of this because this woman was expected to be one of the worst enemies the Eldadorian Emperor could have. She would hate Rancor Mordetur for how her life had turned out – she could be expected to have no love for the daughter of the woman who'd shamed her. This woman had actually *held* Lee in her arms - she could be expected to recognize the daughter of Fovea's other Emperor.

Lee put her head down and focused on her bare toes.

Jing Wei stepped up to Hectaro and regarded him, kneeling in the wet sand by the bank. She took his chin in her hand, her long, red nails pressing into the skin of his face, and looked into his brown eyes.

"This one is a Wolf Soldier," she said. "It is pointless to beat him - he'll die before he tells us why he's here, if he even knows. The Eldadorian Emperor is too crafty to inform a spy of why he's spying. He knows what we'll do if such a person is caught."

Jing Wei stepped over to Lee next. Lee focused on her feet, tried to control her breathing, tried not to sweat. To her left Singer nickered, then Bastard next to her. The stocky Confluni soldiers standing next to them shook their reins.

Lee felt the long, red fingernails under her jowl. Jing Wei forced her head up and looked into her eyes, searching them without empathy, trying to look past them into her soul.

"This one is *not* a Wolf Soldier," she said. "She is our gateway. He either has feelings for her, or he is here to protect her. Either way, we use this one to find out what we want to know."

She pushed Lee's face away and turned to face the Confluni warriors. "Strip them," she said. "Put them in a cart together, we'll carry them to Jeng Chao."

Lee felt a sharp pain as the Princess' hand struck the side of her head. "That will take a week," she said. "In that time, we'll have from them what we need to know, and they will tell my husband why the Emperor is interested now in Conflu."

***

The Princess spoke and her warriors acted - Lee had to give them that.

She was pulled to her feet and her clothes pulled off, Hectaro beside her. Rough hands ran over her skin, through her hair, and finally below her waist. She felt her buttocks pulled open and the heat of a torch held as someone, some *male*, made sure she hadn't used her nether regions to hide a weapon.

From there she was bound wrists and ankles, Hectaro as well, and the two of them loaded into an ox cart next to each other, turned to place Hectaro's sex lay in proximity to her own.

Meanwhile, the other boats which had pursued them were sent polling their way back to the city from whence they'd come. Jing Wei didn't thank them and in fact barely acknowledged their help. Lee came to believe the other Princess had been on some sort of vacation in wilderness, and this event had ruined it for her.

Finally the cart was covered as the sun rose in the east, and the troop was on its way.

Bastard and Singer were tied to the back of the ox cart and, by some miracle, no one tried to ride them. Confluni weren't great equestrians and Lee knew Bastard would allow no one else on his back other than Hectaro. Singer was another matter, but wouldn't be kind to an inexperienced rider.

Hectaro looked into her eyes in the ox cart. It would have been smarter to put them back-to-back, making conversation more difficult, but she had to think instead the Confluni wanted to humiliate Hectaro.

After he spent a day with his privates on hers, she had to imagine they'd make him watch as the soldiers took turns on her. Rather than allow such an act to happen, Hectaro would do whatever they wanted, tell them anything they wanted to know.

Then they'd do it anyway to make sure he wasn't holding anything back.

Then they would kill her – because if she were left alive and word of this got back to her father, he'd burn Conflu to the dirt, kill everyone in it slowly and then salt the earth as a lesson to the rest of Fovea and to assuage his own guilt.

"I don't suppose you can loosen our bindings," Hectaro asked her, his voice barely a whisper.

She shook her head. She'd depleted her magic and she needed food and rest to regain her strength.

"You know what the Confluni do to prisoners," he told her – there was no question; they'd been trained by the same tutors.

She nodded.

"If we tell them who we are –" he began.

Lee shook her head. "That woman is the princess Jing Wei," she said. "Before my father married my mother –"

"I know who Jing Wei is," Hectaro said. "I was also *at* the coronation."

"I'd die before I gave the Confluni a hostage from the Imperial family," Lee said. She looked him in the eye and added, "I'd like to think you feel the same, Wolf Soldier."

He didn't answer, but straightened and didn't look away. Finally she cast her eyes down and closed them. The ox cart wasn't a pleasant ride and her breasts constantly rubbed Hectaro's chest, where thick, dark hair was rough on them and randomly brought them erect. He had his own problems in that area and, as he fought for his own self-control, she tried to avoid thoughts of what was to come.

Her mother had taught her, "Meditate – a sorceress' answers are usually inside of her brain if she could find them." As the ox cart bumped and the prince beside her grumbled and the sun beat down on the canvas over them, stewing them slowly in their own sweat, she drifted into her inner mind, her inner peace – the place where magic dwells and wisdom forms it.

Into the black that had brought her here, into the turmoil of a life barely begun.

"Hello, little one," she heard in her mind.

Her heart constricted. She knew the voice, but the woman who owned it had no power, certainly none like this.

"Who is this?" she demanded – knowing already but just as sure she could not trust the source.

A chuckle in her mind. "I'm an old family friend," she said.

Lee almost lost her concentration, but with an effort bore down on it, on the image of the red-haired woman who'd taken her and her mother captive outside of Thera.

"How is this possible?" Lee demanded.

"The dark isn't just the province of those who cast spells," the woman, Genna, informed her. "It is accessible by those who think deep thoughts, if they think them right."

Some believed those who suffered the black mind dwelt in the dark between, Lee knew. Some also believed those who were mad could come here.

Lee could believe Genna, her father's former lover, was mad.

"Have you enjoyed my little presents?" the woman pressed her. "Have you thrived, because of them?"

Lee immediately knew what Genna meant. The notes she'd received from the things she'd called back from Eldador. If Genna were in Eldador and her parents were not, then the entire Empire might be in danger.

A bump from the ox cart, barely registered in her mind detached from her physical body, reminded her she didn't want for danger.

"Yes," she said, simply. Genna would have a plan – a reason to contact her. If she had a want, then she might still be able to aid her as well.

"Thank you," she forced herself to add.

In the dark she sensed the other woman beaming. "I help you, then you can help me, yes?"

In her mind, Lee shook her head. She couldn't know how such an action would be transmitted in the dark. "I can barely help myself right now," she said, and she told the other woman of her situation.

This broke every rule she'd ever lived by, but she was running out of things to lose. If Genna was anything, even if she were an enemy to her father, she was also a survivor.

The other woman was quiet for long moments – long enough for Lee to believe she'd been abandoned, cast aside as a dead end. Finally, Genna's mind spoke to her with clear urgency.

"I know you're aware of what you're in for," Genna informed her. "You know what the Confluni will do. I can't think your mother hasn't discussed this sort of thing with you: it is at least as common among the tribes of her own people."

In fact, Shela had sat Lee down within days of her becoming a woman. To say she was in any way prepared, though – Lee was terrified of what these Confluni men would do to her, and mortified by the idea Hectaro would be forced to watch it.

"If you identify yourself, I can't think Jing Wei would order any sort of treatment on her own," Genna added. "More likely she'll kill your man and bring you back to the Confluni capital, to be married to a Confluni war lord. Then you'll have the same, but from just one man, and not for weeks."

Lee admitted to herself this hadn't even occurred to her.

"Reach out around you," Genna continued. "Use your mind – see if you can't find this familiar you've cultivated."

"I'm almost drained of my power," Lee protested.

"It won't take much," Genna countered.

Lee detached herself from the dark and reached out around her for the fox. With a mental effort like lifting an anvil, she pressed out past the walls of the ox cart, past the road, past the bushes lining it, to the trees beyond.

She found the fox. It was shadowing them, waiting.

"I have it," she said.

"You have friends you didn't know you had," Genna informed her. "Let the fox know your need, and to go west. It won't have to go far."

"I – I don't," Lee began to argue.

"Just obey me, girl," Genna pressed her. "I've little time left."

Lee transmitted her situation and her instructions to the fox. It was out of her range in a moment.

"It ran away," Lee said.

Lee sensed Genna nodding. "You owe me now, girl," the older woman informed her. "You have a debt to me."

"I know it," Lee admitted. She didn't know if it would matter. She'd likely be dead before the sun rose tomorrow.

"Then this is it – I sense my time here on this world grows nigh," Genna said. "Eveave has *given* to me too handily. I fear the *take*."

Before Lee could add anything, Genna said, "When I am gone, I'm going to need you to aid a good young man, your brother."

This made no sense. "Vulpe?" she asked.

Genna chuckled. "No, dear heart," Genna said, "your other brother. You've more than one, you know."

No, Genna thought, she did *not* know. Her mother had given her father only three children.

"You think yourself you father's oldest child," Genna said, "but you are in fact far from it. There are two older than Lee Mordetur, both boys."

Bastards? Her father had bastards? The love he held for her mother was the stuff of songs – Lee couldn't imagine him betraying his wedding vows.

But then, children older than Lee could have been conceived before he even *met* Shela.

"His name is Lupennen," Genna told her. "He is your half brother.

"My son."

Chapter Twenty-Seven

Friends Unknown

The sun was setting when the ox cart stopped. Lee jolted awake when the canvas cover flew back from over them and the cooler air hit her sweat-covered skin.

Jing Wei stood at the foot of the ox cart, still wearing the same red silk gown, flanked by stout Confluni warriors in leather breast guards.

"Have them out of there," she said in the language of Men.

They were pulled out by their ankles, the rough cart boards ravaging their exposed skin. Each was turned until they were sitting on the back of the ox cart, and then each was pulled to their feet. Lee felt her knees start to give and then the Confluni warrior taking her by her hair to keep her standing.

Hectaro managed to keep his feet under him.

Jing Wei gave an order to one of the Confluni and the man nodded and left them, heading to the front of the cart. She turned back to the two of them, regarding their naked bodies with her index finger on the side of her chin.

"I feel as if I should know the two of you," she said, finally. "It has bothered me – I am very talented in recognizing faces."

Neither Lee nor Hectaro spoke. Lee tried to get a sense of how much of her power she had recovered, however her physical body remained weak from exertion and hunger, making her metaphysical strength hard to gage.

The man returned with a coiled whip, which he handed to the Princess. Jing Wei took it from him and dismissed him with a flick of her wrist.

"A whip like this will part the skin on a bull's back," she said. "I've seen it used to kill a man.

"It will permanently ruin this girl," she added, looking into Hectaro's face. "Before you can beg me to have my man stop, the girl will be a cripple. Do you want that?"

Hectaro stared at her blankly, saying nothing. They'd been schooled in this, as well, as nobles. If captured, give the questioner nothing. Sometimes the torturer needed to work himself up to his greatest efforts – at others, it was a semantics game to make the questioned believe they had given themselves up already. In either case, silence was the safest path.

"So you don't care, then?" she asked. "Very well, turn the girl around."

Lee was turned around on the ox cart and bent over its open back. She heard the princess give a command in Confluni, and then she heard a man step up behind her.

The man said something to the Confluni princess. Jing Wei chuckled and said, "This man wants to take you before he ruins you – he said your behind is quite beautiful. What say you, Wolf Soldier – would you rather see this woman beaten or violated?"

Lee felt her courage leaving her. This shouldn't be happening – it wasn't fair! Where was her invincible father? Why hadn't her mother found her by now? How could Hectaro not have devised a plan to get her free?

She looked up from the rough boards making up the bed of the ox cart into the grinning faces of yellow-skinned Confluni warriors, each probably hoping Hectaro would decide her being raped was less damaging to her.

Little did a man know!

And then, at the edge of the crowd around her, a head took on a look of surprise and dropped out of her line of sight. She almost couldn't believe it, but she had to. She had to have seen that – someone taken from the edge of the crowd, behind the others, as if by a single warrior or a small group trying to free her.

She reached out with her mind, and she touched her little fox, watching from the bushes.

"Very well then," Jing Wei said from behind her. "If you don't care…"

"It will be the last mistake you ever make, Jing Wei of Conflu," Lee called out.

The laughing faces went bland, all eyes focused on the naked girl with the imperious voice.

"Who are you to use my name," the Confluni Princess demanded.

"Someone who isn't too stupid to recognize you," Lee responded, "but that you could say the same."

Such an insult had to be answered.

"Turn her," Jing Wei demanded.

Rough hands had her back on her feet. She was spun around, a strong fist still in her hair.

"Who are you?" Jing Wei demanded.

Confidence returned to the embattled princess, and with it, a sense of her power. With just a flicker of her metaphysical strength, Lee dissolved the ropes at her wrists and ankles. A second later she did the same for Hectaro.

"Princess Lee Mordetur," she spat, straightening her back. "First-born daughter of the Emperor Rancor Mordetur and the Empress Shela, sorceress of the Andaron Long Manes. You're making more enemies than you can count, princess."

Jing Wei searched Lee's face and then nodded. "Your mother – I see her in you," she said. "But your mother is a sorceress; you're little more than an untrained apprentice."

From the corner of her eye, she saw another man drop, again from the farthest edge of the crowd. How many had she counted? She couldn't remember, and if this Confluni princess saw her eyes moving from warrior to warrior then she would give herself away.

A sorceress is taught to focus – Lee focused on Jing Wei. The more time she could buy, the more warriors would die if her savior could remain uncaught.

"You have no idea of my power," Lee hissed.

Hectaro was rubbing his wrists. A Wolf Soldier would be looking for a way to strike, even if he had to trade his life for her safety. Eventually Hectaro would see what she had seen, and he would leap for the closest sword.

Naked with an unfamiliar blade, the veteran Confluni warriors would make short work of him.

Jing Wei chuckled. "Your power seems to have been to sit all day, naked in an ox cart," she countered. Her eyes flickered to the warriors around her, then back to Lee. "I know Andarons are born whores, but an Eldadorian Princess –"

Some insults could be borne, some could not. Lee was tired, frustrated, desperate. She was far from home; she longed for her mother, her father, the cold stone safety of the palace walls in Galnesh Eldador.

Lee focused her will. The red silk gown flew up over the princess' head, exposing her from toes to shoulders, catching up around her arms and enveloping her long, black hair.

Jing Wei screamed. What was humiliating to an Andaron was mortifying to a Confluni, who most likely had only been seen completely naked by her mother and her servants in all of her life.

Confluni warriors pulled their swords. Two ran to the Princess' side. Another fell at the periphery.

Lee took a quick accounting. Eight. There were eight warriors left.

She softened the soil around them, searched it for running water underground and found one spring. She forced the water to rise and mixed it with the earth at the feet of the Confluni.

Hectaro leapt for the warrior nearest him, wrestling for his sword. The mud at the Confluni's feet betrayed both of them as they fell together in a pile, another of the warriors leaping after.

D'leer stood up at the periphery of guards. D'leer, whom they'd left with the Scitai. Somehow she must have found their trail, or perhaps her own logic guided her in the same direction.

Another warrior fell to her sword. Lee raised her right hand, the white power flickering. Her mother would have taken the group of them by now – Lee doubted she would last a minute in the fight.

Better to make it count.

The Confluni princess pushed her gown back into place, Lee found Jing Wei's long, black hair with her magic and made a rope of it, wrapped it around the woman's neck.

Jing Wei gagged. D'leer shouted some command in the Confluni language.

All heads turned to the princess, and then five swords hit the mud, followed by the body of the warrior who'd squared off on the Uman Wolf Soldier.

Hectaro!

Lee couldn't search for the Duke's son *and* maintain her concentration on the princess. She already felt her power slipping. "D'leer!" she commanded, "take the Princess."

Through gritted teeth she added, "Be quick."

D'leer pushed her way past three of the Confluni warriors to stand up behind the choking Jing Wei. Lee released her magic as D'leer's left hand replaced the hair noose at the Princess' throat.

Almost at her feet, she saw a mud-covered Hectaro pushing himself up from the mud, a red stain at his left hip. One uninjured Confluni stood next to him, leaving his sword. Another remained face-down in the mud and would move no more.

"Hectaro!" Lee hissed.

The young man shook his head. "Just a scratch," he said, shaking his head. He tried to smile and to cover the wound with his left hand, but Lee knew better. The slash was bleeding, inches long and right to the bone, packed with mud.

In fact, the mud packing might be the only thing keeping the young man standing.

"To the ox-cart," she ordered him. There was a whip at one of the warriors' feet. She almost stepped to pick it up and then remembered herself. If she put herself within reach of one of these, she might find herself in the middle of a standoff of prisoners.

"D'leer, to the ox cart with Hectaro," she commanded. "The rest of you, back over there, kneel in a line."

D'leer both moved and repeated Lee's orders. Hectaro limped to the bare boards of the bed of the ox cart and leaned against it, unable or unwilling to pull himself up into it. The Confluni soldiers just looked at each other.

Lee raised a hand and forced it to glow white for a moment. Fear of her magic got them moving, and almost brought her to her knees.

A squad of Wolf Soldiers would have surmised the situation and struck already. Lee couldn't manage this many prisoners and couldn't travel any farther today. These warriors lives would end soon, and their charge soon after, or she'd become a prisoner. No Mordetur didn't know what being a prisoner meant since Lee's mother had been captured by the Uman-Chi a dozen years ago. Wolf Soldiers would *never* let a Mordetur be captured again.

Confluni were sworn to die for their liege lord. If it meant another moment's life for Jing Wei, they'd squat in the mud and let Lee or D'leer execute them.

She turned her attention to Jing Wei. "Tell them to strip off their shirts," she said.

Jing Wei simply looked down and D'leer shook her. By then they'd attained the ox cart, and Hectaro had a hand on D'leer's shoulder.

Jing Wei gave them a command, and the group of warriors pulled their shirts off. D'leer turned the Princess over to Hectaro and used them to bind their hands behind their backs, covering their fingers in the process, then each set of wrists to an ankle.

Andarons did this – it wasn't impossible to escape, but it would take hours.

D'leer returned to Lee and the bleeding Prince. She took Jing Wei back from Hectaro and gripped her tight by the hair, at the base of her skull, with her left hand.

"A surprise to see you," Lee said, as her fox trotted out of the bushes and leapt up onto the ox cart.

"Thank that thing," D'leer said, pointing to the fox. "I don't know who or what he is, but he crossed my path hours ago, bold as brass, and then kept trying to lead me off in this direction. At first I thought to kill him, then my curiosity got the better of me."

"Good that it did," Hectaro grunted. He put a hand on Lees shoulder and pushed himself up high enough to sit on the back of the ox cart. Blood was seeping down his left leg, washing away the mud without which he'd be completely naked.

Lee lacked even mud to cover her, she realized. After a day spent naked, she barely missed her clothes, however all eyes were on her.

"Our clothes?" she asked Jing Wei.

The princess snickered. "A long walk for you," she countered. "By then, the daughter of the Emperor will have quite a peasant's tan."

"Yes," Lee said, "I imagine she will. Such a scandal for your father."

Jing Wei's mouth dropped open. Clearly she hadn't even considered Lee might take *her* clothes, however the young girl and full-grown princess were close in size.

"I – I, you cannot!" she stammered.

"If you do," D'leer said, "then you won't have to worry about these following you. Shame her like a whore and she'll take her own life as soon as she gets the opportunity and, if she doesn't and you leave these alive, then they will."

Lee nodded. She might need a prisoner, which made it pointless to render her valueless. She knew better than to leave these warriors in her wake and, after what she'd gone through with the Scitai family, a bunch of Confluni warriors who wanted to take turns on her weren't going to blacken what she felt was her darkening soul.

She pulled herself up on the cart. "Take care of them," she ordered D'leer, "then give me the reins for our horses, and start the ox cart moving east."

D'leer nodded. The Confluni warriors began to pull at their bindings, but D'leer was a veteran Wolf Soldier and had tied her share of captive warriors. When they were dead, D'leer cut away two of the shirts binding them and threw them to Lee. Lee used them to staunch the bleeding from Hectaro's thigh, the young man already becoming light headed, blinking and trying to focus his eyes.

Jing Wei smiled almost evilly. "That man is already dead," she said. "His body just doesn't know it."

Lee wanted to slap the other Princess but dared not waste the strength. D'leer returned with the two horses and handed the reins to Lee. She then took Jing Wei by the hair and dragged her to the front of the ox cart.

Two oxen could pull a cart for a long time, especially one as lightly loaded as this. The sun approaching the western horizon, Lee also didn't fear for one of the beasts stepping in a hole. Their legs were thicker than hers.

Moving slowly, the horses would be as safe as could be expected behind the cart. Lee didn't want to go far, just far enough to distance herself from the bodies, to find a safer place to sleep and to recover. She told D'leer as much as the cart started moving forward, after tying the reins of each horse to opposite sides of the back of the cart.

She looked for food and found a wooden box filled with it. Not her usually jerked meat and dried vegetables, she found fare more fit for a Princess, boiled chicken spiced and held in leaves, once-steamed vegetables and wine.

She gave the wine to Hectaro and she stuffed the chicken into her mouth. She and the fox ate ravenously, passing a share to D'leer and leaving a good pile for the fox who'd saved her.

Finally, she addressed Hectaro.

She focused her mind, found the wound inside of him. She began the process of knitting the flesh, reconnecting the veins. She hoped the wine would replenish him, or at least let him rest and heal. She had become more familiar with the young man, and familiarity made healing him easier.

Which was a good thing, because she passed out doing what she could.

Chapter Twenty-Eight

The Loss of Youth, Goals and Life

In her mind, Lee was back in between with Vedeen, as she'd been what seemed to be years ago when Hectaro had saved her from Angron Aurelias.

Could it really have been just a month?

She had no way to be sure – of anything.

"What have we here?" the Druid's voice, falsely sweet, asked her. "The daughter of the Emperor, back in the black?"

"I'm," Lee began, and then collected herself. "I'm near where you left me."

"And the worse for wear," the Druid commented. "While an Empire burns from within, and an Emperor rages for vengeance over a daughter's death, thinking he has but one more."

The riddles from the Druid made Lee's head spin. She'd pushed herself too far. This was likely all a fever dream, and not a good one.

"Do you remember what I promised you?" Vedeen asked Lee. "Do you remember the price of my assistance?"

Lee remembered the dying curse from the Scitai woman before Hectaro killed her and her children. Lee remembered their cold, staring eyes before she covered them in river silt.

The Druid read these images from the surface of Lee's mind, and recoiled.

"You swore I'd lose my youth before its time," Lee said. "You swore Hectaro would lose his goals, and D'leer her life."

"I can see you're well on your way to losing more than you dreamed!" Vedeen said. "Such – atrocity. To visit such things on innocents."

Lee had to wonder, feeling as she did right then, if there was even such a thing as an innocent.

"*You* try and survive here," Lee shot back at the Druid. "You try and live among those who hate you for your heritage, for the color of your skin, the shape of your eyes. I'm both an Eldadorian and an Andaron in *Conflu*, Druid. What do you expect of me, except atrocity?"

Vedeen probed her mind, and found the volcano she'd created, the people she'd killed, the theft, the pain delivered to innocents, to animals.

She said what Lee herself had thought about herself, "You have truly earned the name Mordetur."

For Lee to think it was one thing. To hear it from the one she blamed for causing it was another. From within her, a frustration and a violence swelled.

She felt the Druid retreating and Lee held the other woman in place with her will.

"A Mordetur?" she demanded. "A Mordetur? Is that what I am? Is a Mordetur what you fear?"

And Lee poured out all of the rage, all of the grief, the fear, the frustration of the weeks spent on the run in Conflu. She directed it all like a cyclone, and she unloaded it on the unprepared Druid.

The other's scream shook the *æther*, reverberating against Lee. The Druid struggled like a trapped animal to be free of the sorceress.

The result was Lee leaping up, naked and fully awake, from the back of the ox cart.

Before she realized where she was, she raised her hand to the East, and she released her power, scorching the air, seeking an enemy no longer there.

"War's whiskers," Hectaro swore.

D'leer leapt up and pulled her sword. It was night and they'd made themselves a fire. D'leer had found the unconscious group of them a space among hills to the West of the Jeng-Jeng River and picketed their animals.

A fortunate thing, because the oxen snorted and pulled at their tethers, the horses struggling against their hobbles. Jing Wei awoke screaming.

White power ripped the night, announcing to anyone for a full twenty daheeri who wasn't blind, "There is a sorceress here!"

"Lee!" Hectaro admonished her.

Lee tried to rein in the power, but it ran free with no spell or incantation to control it. Instead of trying to draw it back in, she cycled it into something she needed.

Clothes. She and Hectaro needed something to wear. Pulling unfamiliar items from Galnesh Eldador should absorb all of this power.

She reached for her personal closet, and she found herself there. Not just seeking in spirit this time, she felt the cold wooden floor on her feet, smelled the familiar, horsey musk of her personal possessions, and knew she was in her room.

In her room, with a red-haired woman dressed in tight, black leather. The woman looked up guiltily from a pile of Lee's private writings at her desk, surprised and dismayed to see the naked princess.

"Well, this is unexpected," she said. "What brings you naked to the halls of your father's palace?"

"I," Lee began, and stumbled. "That is, we – Hectaro and D'leer and I –"

The red-head stood and raised a hand to silence her. "You aren't really here, are you?" she asked. "This is some witchery?"

Lee looked around her. She couldn't be sure.

The red-head ran to Lee's armoire and returned with a white blouse, a leather blue cape, black leather riding pants and a pair of riding boots.

"Quickly," she said. "Take this. Magix like this must be taxing for you."

Lee took them. At first they started to pass through her forearms, as if she were a ghost, but she focused her will and took them, felt them soft against her skin.

"Hectaro," she said. "The Duke's son. He – I, nothing. No clothes."

The woman nodded and was out the door. Lee felt her essence starting to dissolve, the magic spending itself.

There would be ramifications for this.

Impossibly fast, Genna was back with more clothing. She forced them into Lee's arms.

"Remember," she said. "Remember you have another brother. My son."

"What?"

The air was becoming misty. She could see this woman before her, and she could feel Hectaro's hands on her shoulders, shaking her. She could see D'leer standing behind him.

"Lupennen," the red-head said. "Son of Clear Genna. Son of Lupus the Conqueror. Your brother. Your *other* brother.

"Remember that!"

And then Lee was back in Conflu, and the world was dark again – darker than the void before.

***

Lee awoke again in the middle of the day, the sun warm on her face, her clothes hot against her skin.

Her stomach hurt so badly she doubled over from the pain and could only groan.

Hectaro appeared at her side with fresh venison. She took it and devoured it, and again when he brought more. She drank some wine and ate another grown man's portion before she felt well enough to sit upright in the back of the ox cart.

They'd moved again. This wasn't where they'd been when she'd awoken in the night. Already, those events didn't seem real, except she wore the clothes Clear Genna had handed to her.

D'leer had stopped the ox cart. The look on her face said something had been going on, and it had the Wolf Soldier squad leader worried.

"What's happening with you?" Hectaro asked her.

Lee shook her head. "I pushed too far," she said. Then she remembered why she'd done it. "Your leg?" she demanded.

"My hip, really," Hectaro corrected her and, standing, he raised and lowered his right knee. "See – you did a great job. Better than the day I was born."

Lee knew better. She just hadn't had the time to do a proper job, however Hectaro was moving, and moving meant, "Not dead," and for the condition she was in, "not dead" in and of itself was quite an accomplishment.

She studied the clothes he wore for a moment.

"Those are my father's," she said, finally.

Hectaro nodded. "And your father is a big man," he said, "but with some tucking in, I fit them and at least I'm not naked anymore."

"You brought them to him," D'leer said. "How could you not know?"

Lee took a moment and brought them up to speed in her night's travels through the here and in between. As she did so, D'leer got the ox cart moving east again, and Hectaro leapt on to Bastard's bare back. Singer walked along behind the ox cart, her reins still tied to one of its hand rails.

"You're going to wish you hadn't done that, I think," D'leer informed her without turning in her seat.

"Oh, you can count on that," Jing Wei informed them all. "You will soon be meeting my father, and many members of the Imperial Guard, the fighting elite of Conflu."

Lee knew of the Imperial Guard – the fighting elite of the Confluni National Guard, who protected the Emperor and his family. Her father had explained to her families in power much, like he with his Wolf Soldiers, usually chose an elite for themselves.

Unlike many of them, her father often recycled those warriors back into common ranks now and again, in order to keep them sharp as well as to spread their abilities. They hadn't done this with D'leer, and she'd capitalized on her position in ways that hadn't helped the Mordeturs.

Wizards were rare among the Confluni. She knew her demonstration, especially at night, was going to bring investigation. If someone could calculate its origin came from the vicinity of Jing Wei's last known location, then it could easily bring the Imperial Guard.

"How badly do we need this ox cart?" she asked D'leer.

The Wolf Soldier squad leader turned in her seat, the way before her nothing more than an open plain with little to navigate around.

"It's packed with food," she said. "Enough for her personal guard and herself for several days, which means a *long* time for us. They've got bows, arrows, all packed away and available.

"As well," D'leer said, turning back around, "your saddles were lost with your boat. You're going to be able to ride a little faster on your horses, but we all can't."

Lee nodded. The sky told her they were going straight east, and her memory told her she was practically parallel to the Jeng-Jeng River, closing on it slowly.

If they were left alone, they could stay away from those farming communities surely existing along a fresh-water river and find a boat past the city to the east of Jeng Chao. From there they had a good chance of making it to Wisex, and from there anything could be possible.

But they weren't going to be left alone, and the ox cart moved barely faster than a warrior could walk. The warriors wouldn't be walking, and if they had those ponies...

The worst part was they needed to make their decision now. Once they were seen, even if they left the Princess and mounted and rode, the ponies would have no trouble keeping up with them.

Lee reached out into Earth around her, the fox immediately leaping up into her lap from somewhere beside the cart as she focused. She stroked his fur and searched for the marching feet of soldiers, the rough feel of someone moving fast through dirt.

She'd never done this before – not this way. Where she'd had trouble before, now she was sensing all manner of insects, rodents, small animals and even birds pecking at worms and ant hills around her. She tried to tune them out, but where once she'd lacked the power for what she wanted, now it seemed she had too much.

Her first instinct was to push the fox out of her lap but she disregarded it. Instead, in her mind, she *became* the fox, out in the plains, running free, looking at all of the things she could see.

Immediately she thought to devour the mice, to chase the birds, but she held her instinct back. She raced out to the west, back across their path, where danger would be coming from.

Back to the hills where she'd woken up the night before, she found them – no less than fifty warriors, their faces flushed from running; a small group with bald heads and black-and-white pony tails, dressed in white robes with yellow belts, searching around the site, picking up stones, whispering to each other.

She roved out a little farther and found six ponies – enough for the white robes. There were tracks for more, but not many. Maybe another half-dozen.

As she called her will back to her body, she considered the Emperor or whomever was looking for Jing Wei had made a critical error. They'd sent too many – even if the ones on horseback found them, they were at best six wizards and six warriors. The mainstay of their force would hold them back from finding them as quickly as they could.

When she was back in her own body, none the worse for wear, she focused her attention on Jing Wei, who'd turned her face to watch her.

This had been a pretty girl once, Lee thought. Time had been hard on her. She'd suffered disgrace and embarrassment, then the indignity of being tossed as a reward to someone who would replace the Emperor of Conflu, probably without a word to her.

She could see all of this in the lines of her face, in the gray starting to touch her hair.

"Your wizards dress in white robes, with gold belts?" she asked the other Princess.

Jing Wei squinted her eyes. "Why?"

"Answer the question," Lee demanded, straightening.

Jing Wei straightened in turn.

"Strike her," Lee ordered D'leer.

With no other provocation, the Uman Wolf Soldier's fist flew from the reins of the ox cart to the side of the Confluni Princess' face. The dull thud of a fist against a head followed, then D'leer was back to guiding the cart as if nothing had happened.

The Confluni's jaw dropped and her hands flew to her face. Lee was surprised the Princess hadn't been bound, but then thought again. Why bother? She wouldn't fight – she was raised as an object.

Tears of indignation welled in her eyes.

"Shall we do that again?" Lee asked.

Jing Wei's eyes flickered from Lee to D'leer, her courage fleeing her. She'd likely never been struck in her life.

"There is a sect of very good wizards living in mountains by Shin Dee," she said. "They came recently to Jeng Chao. They ride, and they cast."

Lee nodded.

"Is that who we have after us?" D'leer asked.

"I believe so," Lee said. "How long have we been on the road today?"

D'leer looked at sun, then back at the trail. "Three hours," she said.

"Then that's how far behind us they are," she said. "The wizards, and some mounted scouts. Fifty warriors on foot, running."

Hectaro trotted up to the side of the cart, concern on his face. "We have trouble," he said.

"Can never have enough of that," D'leer replied, still looking forward.

Lee sighed. "Turn to the northeast," she said.

D'leer twitched the reins and the oxen turned about thirty degree to their left. Hectaro plodded alongside on Bastard, and the other Princess sobbed, occasionally touching her fingers to the swollen spot by her cheek.

Lee studied the ground behind them, picking out the details of the ox cart tracks, two rough lines, parallel to each other.

With a minor exercise of her will, the ruts filled back in with the dirt displaced by the wooden wheels. For one daheer behind them, then two, then three, the ruts disappeared like wrinkles from a sheet pulled tight across a table, leaving no evidence.

A moment later, and with considerably more effort, the horse tracks filled in as well, and then those of the oxen. Where she could eliminate the ruts in a sweep, the hoof marks had to be pursued one-at-a-time; a fraction of the power, but thousands of times over.

But she wasn't done yet.

She released the little fox and in her mind instructed it to find the end of the cart tracks. She could still see the animal's tail with her naked eyes when the fox found what she was seeking, then sat and looked back over its shoulder at her.

Lee bore down, and she drove the cart tracks for two more daheeri east, and then followed those with the appropriate hoof prints. As the fox ran back to her, she felt her mind begin to waver and her stomach growl for nourishment.

The fox leapt up into the back of the cart, curling up in Lee's lap. The younger Princess thought for a moment she should sleep before she tried to eat again, when she noticed something in the fox's mouth.

She reached for it, and the fox released a piece of silk, the color of the robe Jing Wei was wearing. Lee sighed and held it up for Hectaro to see, and then called for D'leer's attention.

D'leer shook her head. "Strip her?" she asked.

The Confluni Princess clutched at the front of her robes, revealing the end of a shredded sleeve, where she'd clearly been extracting pieces.

Lee shook her head. "Bind her," she said. She reached into one of the wooden containers built against the front of the ox cart, and pulled out a wedge of cheese.

"Don't unbind her again," she said.

D'leer nodded, tucked the reins to one side of her seat and turned to Jing Wei.

To their combined shock, the Confluni Princess leapt for the side of the ox cart – not to escape, but to pitch her body underneath it.

No magic Lee was capable of could have stopped her, however D'leer was closer and needed none. She pushed the Princess wide of her goal but, in the process, fell herself where Jing Wei had tried to go.

The left side of the ox cart rose and fell with a sick crunch.

Hectaro leapt from Bastard and had the Princess by the hair as she tried to throw herself back into the cart's path. Jing Wei struggled against him, but he simply drew her back to him by her long, black hair until he could take her by the arms.

Lee leapt for the cart reins and stopped the two oxen. She turned southwest and saw D'leer holding her middle, lying on her side in an ox cart rut, blood staining the ground around her.

Lee tied off the reins and leapt out of the back of the cart, running to the Uman Wolf Soldier's side. The training her mother had given her as a healer took over.

Lee squatted at D'leer's side and pushed her shoulder back, exposing her middle. The ox cart had pinned her to the dirt and the ground down across her body. Lee pushed back the remains of D'leer's clothes to see torn skin and, past the ruined flesh, smashed organs, broken ribs and no shortage of blood.

She focused her will and stopped the bleeding, trying to restitch the organs, to reknit the bones.

D'leer grunted, turned her head from side-to-side, then screamed in pain. Hectaro's and Lee's own heads rose, looking to the horizon for the Confluni soldiers who would come to the call of the dying Wolf Soldier.

D'leer gripped Lee's shoulder for strength.

"Magic is no miracle," she gasped, searching for Lee's eyes with her own. When they met, Lee immediately saw what her mother would have called 'the dying look.' A warrior knows what his or her body is capable of healing, and D'leer was well past her limit.

Even if Lee could repair the other's broken body, the pain would kill her. She extended her will instead to block the pain running from the destroyed organs to D'leer's brain, in what her father had described to her as a nerve system. He'd called it a system like tiny torches, blinking messages through paths in the body.

Lee extinguished the torches. D'leer sighed and settled back into the road.

"Thank you," she said.

Lee shook her head. Hectaro was already forcing Jing Wei back into the cart. "I've done nothing for you," the Princess said. "I've simply stopped the pain."

"And for that, I thank you," D'leer said. "As much as any Wolf Soldier could ask of a Mordetur."

A tear rolled down the side of Lee's face. "Why, D'leer?" she demanded, finally. "Why betray us? What did my father do to you, that you would turn his daughter over to the King of Trenbon."

D'leer sighed. She looked to the west, then back to Lee, and finally took her hand away from the other's shoulder.

Looking into the sky, away from Lee, she said, "The first service of a Wolf Soldier is to Lupus," she said.

"Lupus seeks to rally all of the Fovean nations under his banner. He'll rally them by taking all of the ports on Tren Bay. I learned this – as a part of the inner circle, as one of his most trusted guards.

"For one with a Man's years, it seems a good plan," she continued, and then licked her dry lips. "But for one with an Uman's gift of Life, the problem doesn't come with the taking of the land, even the keeping of it. The problem comes with the prize such land is – the others who would step in on Lupus' accomplishment."

"You mean the Uman-Chi?" Lee asked, referring to the long-lived descendants of the Cheyak. The Uman-Chi King was almost one thousand years old, and for members of their race to live to seven hundred was not unheard of.

D'leer shook her head. "Angron Aurelias surely believes he could step in after your father's natural death. If he lived another fifty years, five decades is nothing to an Uman-Chi.

"But your father is the instrument of the god War," she said, "and the god War is a capricious god. We Uman know that the race of Men is not his favorite.

"At least," she said, her voice becoming more of a croak as her life's blood left her, "not the race of Eldadorian Men."

Lee straightened. In the ox cart, Hectaro had bound Jing Wei's hands and feet, and was tying her by her hair to the hand rail, braiding it so it would take another rescuer long minutes to release her.

Lee had studied the gods as a part of her tutelage. She knew, while the Elder gods, Adriam and Eveave, even Earth and Water, Power and Desire, were usually more interested in the furtherance of Life's children, in fact the children of Power and Desire, War, Destruction and Chaos, tended to serve themselves, and saw all living things as tools, and nothing more.

Somehow, D'leer had foreseen War's machinations weren't in Lupus' best interests, and serving him meant betraying him, delaying his goal of a united Fovea.

A Fovea would be so easy to hand off to another, if War willed it. Especially after a weakening war.

Lee stood as a final sigh left the injured Wolf Soldier's body. She'd called D'leer a traitor, but perhaps D'leer had been the most loyal Wolf Soldier of all.

Chapter Twenty-Nine

Fast Flight

Lee Mordetur, Princess of Eldador, Andaron Sorceress, stepped into the ox cart from its rear tailgate, unbound her mare's reins from its handles and, drawing her to the side of the cart, leapt up onto her back. The skittish mare, much the worse-for-wear for its time in Conflu, side stepped before a tug on her reins settled her.

Lee turned her to face Hectaro, standing next to the bound Princess in the cart.

"Take as much of their supplies as you can bundle," she ordered him. "Hand me a bow and two quivers."

Hectaro furrowed his brow. "You shoot?" he asked.

Her mother was an expert with a bow, her brother might be called 'very good.' She herself had little interest in it growing up.

But she may be glad of the opportunity to put a few shafts in the air later.

"Just hand them to me," she said.

Hectaro shrugged and did as he was told. He didn't have saddle bags, but there were four quivers left, and he emptied them of arrows and filled them with sausage, cheese, jerked meat and carrots – most of what was left of their fare. He took two water and two wine skins, and he wrapped the long shoulder straps of each of these together, and laid them evenly across Bastard's rump. He leapt up in front of it all and waited for Lee.

Her little fox companion leapt up into her lap at the same time. Lee made a space for it in front of her, keeping it's claws well away from the horse's hide. Singer might balk at the idea of a predator on her back.

Jing Wei looked up at the other Princess from her ox cart.

"We're leaving you," Lee said. "Perhaps your people will find you, perhaps the crows will, instead.

"If it's your people," she continued, leaning forward, looking right into Jing Wei's eyes, "Then you will do well to get back to your father, and forget about two Eldadorians trying to get home."

Jing Wei looked away and then back at the other Princess, but said nothing.

Lee thought for a moment about just killing her, but she'd killed enough people. If she went her whole life and never killed another, all would be fine with her.

Taking other lives to better her own didn't have the appeal in reality she'd enjoyed in stories.

Lee kicked her mare and turned her to the northeast, Hectaro following her. She didn't look back at the Confluni Princess, even when the girl grew confident and started screaming for help. As she'd said, maybe Jing Wei's people would find her, and maybe it would be the crows.

That couldn't be helped now.

***

It took a day to reach the junction where the Kwon Do River spilled into the Jeng-Jeng, their horses moving in an easy, loping canter they could maintain for daheeri. Once there, they could see the city on the other side of the river, whose name they didn't know.

It was walled like the other ones they'd seen, and boat traffic moved in and out of it, probably from Jeng Chao. No traffic came from the east and, for all of the times Lee's mind had flown across this area, she'd never seen anything to tell her otherwise.

Missing this told her two things: they were close to Andoron, and they'd see little Confluni resistance past this point.

If they could make it to the river.

"Do we steal another barge?" Hectaro asked her. The sun was setting to their west. People would be off of the river soon. There would be more families like the Scitai they'd killed, thinking themselves safe in settled land, so close to a major city.

Lee didn't want to do any more killing, but she had a mission now. D'leer's last words were rolling around in her head. Echoes of their meaning were haunting her. *"...the god War is a capricious god, and we Uman know the race of Men is not his favorite..."*

She took the fox up in her hands and she looked into its eyes. She conveyed to it she wanted another barge like their last one, big enough for the horses, and she dropped the fox on the ground.

She didn't respond to Hectaro, she just watched the fox slink off into the dusk. Through its eyes she saw the gentle terrain turn into plowed fields, rough branch-and-lashwork docks for weary travelers and, here and there, a man or a family selling food and trading with the river people who hadn't made it into the city before its gates closed.

The fox had travelled two daheeri before it came upon a vessel beached in the river sand, an older, deep-drafted junk with a triangular sail and seats for oarsmen. The fox scrabbled over the boat's side to see the rain water in the hull, but not much, and none of the leakage she'd expect if the ship had hit a rock and then been washed up from the river to here.

The boat was beached, its owners had left it, probably meaning to scavenge it later, or perhaps about to do so now. The fox could smell there had been people here hours before.

Lee walked her mare to the stallion's side and, much as she had in the past, she willed the entire boat and fox to her, this time turning the spell to bring the two of them with their mounts to the location of the boat by the river.

Both Bastard and Singer had done this with the Empress before. The stallion hopped up on his back legs as if considering rearing, but didn't. Singer nickered but stayed on the ground.

The fox ran back into the boat, its head emerging comically over the side when nothing came to challenge it.

"What – what?" Hectaro sputtered. He glared at Lee as he settled his mount. He probably had a thousand questions for Lee, but a look from her silenced him. Lee regarded the boat from horseback, then turned her attention up and down the river.

She dismounted, Hectaro after her, and she handed him her reins. "Load the horses," she ordered him without thinking much of it. "Tell me when you're ready and I'll free the boat, and we'll leave for Wisex."

Hectaro grimaced and took the reins.

He'd been her friend. Her protector. To be honest with herself, she'd wanted him for her man for most of her life.

But Hectaro would never be her man. She was a Princess, her father the most powerful Man on Fovea, at least for now. If she meant for Hectaro to keep any of his identity, if she meant for Fovea to stay Fovean, she had to change her thinking.

She had some growing up to do. She had to remind herself that Hectaro, be what he was, was a vassal to her father.

She turned her face to where the Duke's son couldn't see it, and wiped away a final tear for the life she'd lost.

***

The larger boat didn't scare the horses as much, and Hectaro, after failing to get his stallion aboard, loaded Singer instead and then could barely keep Bastard away from the gunwales. He cleared the rowing benches from the back fourth of the ship and then had a manageable stall for the two horses in under two hours.

By then the sun was down and the white light of the moon guided them. With barely a word, Lee entered the boat and then used her will to evacuate the dirt from the riverbed where it held the boat in place. The craft lurched once, tilted dangerously toward the center of the river until what little breeze there was took its sail, and then guided itself almost on its own toward Wisex and out of Conflu.

The boat had a guide handle for its rudder amidship, and several lines for the sail. The latter was tattered along the edges and the bottom, a veteran of too many voyages, but sufficed to keep them moving with the flow of the river. Under cover of night and with no one pursuing them, Lee found herself actually resting for the first time since she'd left the safety of the Imperial palace in Eldador.

The fox curled up at her feet. It had caught itself some sort of large rodent while waiting for Hectaro, and it was feasting on it now.

Lee found herself both starving and not wanting to eat.

"What's wrong with you?" Hectaro finally asked her.

He was seated at a bench behind the guide handle, his eyes on the river, watching for anything that might show up in their way. Lee might be relaxed, but relaxing was a luxury unfit for a Wolf Soldier.

Still, her first thought was to be offended by his impertinence. How dare he? She reined in her emotions as quickly as she felt them. Hectaro wouldn't be a Wolf Soldier forever, and she wasn't done needing him.

"Did you hear D'leer's last words?" Lee asked him.

He nodded. "She feared the world your father is creating, and she thought she had to stop him," he said. "Typical of a traitor to say she's saving us all."

Lee shook her head. Hectaro had missed it. "You heard her call War a capricious god?" she pressed him.

"Yes."

Lee sighed. She wasn't sure how much of this she should share, especially if Hectaro didn't understand it. Again, he wouldn't be a Wolf Soldier forever.

He'd be a Duke. For all she knew, he already *was* one. His father might be cold in his grave.

For that matter, he might be a common, though she doubted her father would appoint another so quickly. War could make almost anything happen.

Which had been D'leer's point.

"My father seeks to unite all of the shores on Tren Bay under an Eldadorian banner," she said, finally.

Hectaro nodded.

"When he succeeds," she continues, "the other Fovean nations will be land-locked, and their sole trading partner will be Eldador. Even Dorkan, if my father wishes it. While they could trade with the outer islands, in fact Eldador will hold the coast of the Forgotten Sea with his Sea Wolves in time, or he'll savage their trading ships so badly he might as well hold it."

"If he doesn't just *take* the outer islands," Hectaro said.

Lee had considered this as well.

"Because my father is the instrument of War," Lee said. "Just as my mother claims to be the instrument of Power."

Hectaro nodded.

Lee kept waiting for him to make the leap of logic she had made, but it wasn't coming. People claimed her father didn't think the thoughts other people thought, and he'd schooled his children as much as any other had. Perhaps Lee's thinking was more her father's than a Fovean's.

Perhaps she now had an explanation why she felt such urgency to find her way home now.

"Hectaro," Lee said, "D'leer said the race of Men, at least, those of Eldador, were not the favorites of War."

"I heard that, too," he said, and then the idea gave him pause.

Why wasn't War doing this for his favorite people?

Or, worse, what if he *was*? What if her father was just setting the stage for another race to come in, accept it from him and then to rule in his stead?

What would the instrument of War do, when the favorites of War demanded he bend his knee? She asked as much of Hectaro.

The heir to Galnesh Eldador had no answer, and neither did she.

They sailed in silence for a long while.

***

Three days on the Jeng-Jeng River found Lee and Hectaro passing an escarpment to their north, a small series of hills clearly being quarried for the ultra-hard granite it was composed of.

Their time on the river had been unpredictably hard. The horses had fouled the back of the boat repeatedly, making it slick and dangerous for them to be on. Feeding them had proven even more difficult because the boat had no anchor and could only stop by grounding it. When the horses felt the boat grounding, they fought to leap out to dry land, and finally Lee and Hectaro had to just let them do it, stopping at night for them to eat off of the boat while they did what they could to clean and maintain the older craft.

The morning before they found the escarpment, Hectaro pointed out cracks in the hull where they'd started to 'perspire,' meaning while they were just barely leaking now, they would be more severely soon.

At this quarry, one hundred Wolf Soldier guards protected a flat-bed barge, a small team of Dwarves and a Sea Wolf, the *House of Stowe*, out of Galnesh Eldador.

At first sight of them, the Sea Wolf broke away from the shore and bore down on them, more than a dozen Aschire archers at her bow with bows drawn, and at least another Century of Wolf Soldiers with swords drawn, waiting for anything to get past she Aschire.

Lee wanted to weep. She stepped to the bow and spread her arms and legs wide, making an 'X' of her body, a sign among Eldadorians to be recognized where they weren't supposed to be.

A grappling hook sailed out from the side of the Sea Wolf toward their barge. Two attempts were needed before the larger craft could grapple the smaller.

A suspicious-looking Sea Wolf commander stared at them over his higher gunwales. "Well," he said, "I'll believe that yer not Confluni, but I can't say as I know you, either, and there's not many as would come this way out of Conflu."

Lee straightened, but it was Hectaro who spoke. "We are the Princess Lee Mordetur and Hectaro, son of Hectar, Duke of Galnesh Eldador, and we seek succor."

The frown on the Wolf Soldier's face was almost frightening to see. "There's a lot of people who you could've pretended to be, whoever y'are," he drawled, "but you should not have picked them two. Ever'one in the Empire knows that poor Lee died with Hectaro in the first days of Chaos, not six weeks ago."

There was a grumbling among the Wolf Soldiers, and a few of the Aschire pulled their bows a little tighter. The Aschire loved the Emperor and his pain might have been theirs, as far as Lee knew.

But Lee would know that, because she'd spent almost every day of her life in the presence of one of the most famous Aschire of all. She turned to them rather than to the Wolf Soldiers.

In Aschire, she said, "What Eldadorian other than Lee Mordetur would speak your language so perfectly, except for she who was a part of the forest with Nina, daughter of Krell, Duke of the Aschire?"

The already-surprised look natural to the Aschire people became even more surprised when they heard her words. Nina had insisted speaking Aschire would save them one day, and apparently their warden had been right.

One turned to the Wolf Soldier Commander. "Do you have anyone from the first or third Millenium?" he asked. Those were the two thousand Wolf Soldiers who were always stationed at Galnesh Eldador, and who would know the Imperial Family on sight.

The Commander disappeared, and then called to the shore. Five of the Wolf Soldiers there leapt into a row boat and began the stretch out to where the two ships were grappled in the river.

"Is yer last chance, if yer lyin'," the Commander said to Lee and Hectaro. "Ol' Drenten spent a year in the first, and he'll know ya –"

"I know Drenten," Lee interrupted him. "Wanton gambler, loves to drink, has two scars and has been everything from Commander of 100 to a sergeant and back because of it."

The Commander's face split wide in a smile. "'At's 'im" he said. "If ye know Drenten…"

But he went no farther, because by then the row boat had come within eye contact of the Confluni boat, and Drenten with the Princess. He let out a whoop, shucked his sword and leapt into the river, boots, tabard and all.

A more heavily armored man would have found the bottom of the river before the side of the boat, but fortunately for Drenten the armor in this part of the Empire was mostly leather. Drenten swam to the side of their boat, and Hectaro helped him over the gunwale.

"Bless ye," he said, taking the Princess in a bear hug. "Bless ye, bless ye and love ye, my little lady," he repeated, his voice catching in his throat.

Lee had never been hugged by a Wolf Soldier before, but she knew the story of how her uncle had held her up before the assembled Pack and rallied their loyalty to her, before the sack of Outpost IX. Drenten had been there.

She patted him on the back, and he stepped away from her, tears in his eyes unmasked by the river water.

"When I heard word of, well, y'know," Drenten said, his breath reeking of bad teeth and worse whiskey, "I swore if it could not be true, then I'd never touch a drop, never gamble a copper Tabaar again."

He reached into his tunic and took out a flask. Without another word, he threw it into the river. "Be that a price well paid, little lady," he said.

Chapter Thirty

The Black Lake

The Black Lake where the Mid, Safe and Jeng-Jeng Rivers met, sported currents so strong no person alive could swim against them. All things in the Black Lake were eventually swept down into the Mid River, and then into the Slee Nation. The Slee notoriously tortured and ate the hapless fools who suffered this fate and lived.

Lee would have preferred to transfer her horses to the Sea Wolf and then to abandon the Confluni boat, however the only ways to do this would be to use a crane, which they did not have, or to ground both ships on Confluni territory and to perform the transfer there.

Supposedly the Confluni were well-aware of the Eldadorians using these hills as a source of granite, and had already petitioned the city of Wisex to stop doing it. Because they still needed the rock, and the next best source was the Iron Mountains, Eldador had no intention of discontinuing what they were doing, any more than they intended to discontinue felling trees from the Confluni woods along the Black Lake while a timber farm took root and grew in Andoron, just north of the land which Wisex claimed.

Eldador defended the tree farm, too, however the Andarons saw the benefit of thousands of trees to harvest and put up little resistance to the decades-long project. The Confluni saw little benefit in a stronger Wisex.

A dozen Wolf Soldiers took up the benches on the Confluni boat, manned the rigging and replaced the sail, even tarred the hull where the wood was perspiring. After much deliberation, it was decided they could sail the ship alongside the Confluni junk while the barge waited on the other side of the Jeng-Jeng River, then return for it.

"We'd all feel better, were ye aboard the *House of Stowe,* the Commander argued with the Princess. Both she and Hectaro shook their heads.

"Your sailors will have their hands full with the rigging," Hectaro said. "If the horses act up, and it's likely, it will take familiar hands to calm them.

"Bastard is one of Blizzard's sons," he finished. "I'm the only one who can handle him."

"And I won't abandon Singer," Lee said. How could she? The loyal mare had borne her across mountain and plain, through smoke and from flowing lava. Some might say, "Just a horse," but that person bled no Andaron blood.

The Commander nodded. "We'll brace ye, then," he said. "You'll run upwind of us – don't be worried if your hull and ours trades splinters. We'll have ye into port, turn 'round and fetch the barge. Shouldn't take us an hour."

Lee nodded and the two craft took off, letting the Jeng-Jeng move them ever-faster into the Black Lake. Once the Jeng-Jeng tributary opened up, Lee saw the great, obsidian shelf rising up from its center, daheeri wide. The foundation for the great city of Wisex.

She'd been here when this shelf was raised, although she didn't remember it. If her mother and Nina were to be believed, she'd participated in the raising, her magic upholding her mother's strength at the tender age of two years old. At first she'd marveled at the tale, later she'd been skeptical of it, finally she'd just thought it a quaint story meant to encourage a budding Sorceress.

Now she saw the shelf, scarred obsidian thrusting up like a challenge from the churning currents in the Black Lake, and she recognized her handiwork. She didn't remember the act, but she knew the power and she smelled her own signature in the magic.

This is what I can do, she thought to herself. *This is the work of the one who brings volcanoes to life.*

The Confluni ship immediately sidled up alongside of the *House of Stowe* like a scared colt to its mother, the sailors onboard the smaller ship using poles to keep hull damage to a minimum. If the ship broke apart here, there would be no retrieving those on it. The *House* would make for the entrance to the Mid River, turn sideways and hope to snatch those who were washed toward the Slee Nation from the water. They wouldn't even try for the horses.

No, Lee thought to herself. *We don't die here. Not today.*

Both ships turned to the north, to come around the island from the west, and then into her stone and timber harbor. The turn made use of the existing currents to drive them right into port, where they could exit and then abandon the Confluni boat.

It didn't take them minutes to pass the great stone walls, the parapets, the soaring towers of Wisex. Built by Dwarves, it was a city to challenge the might and the beauty of Outpost IX, or Galnesh Eldador or of any other city on Fovea. Her walls stood one hundred feet tall and as much as thirty feet thick at the base, her gates were a hulking mass of steel-bound timbers facing an arcing bridge leading from the Andaron land to the island – a bridge which could support more than three hundred heavy horse, but which could be dropped into the Lake with a single blow of a hammer, if someone knew where to hit it.

The Wolf's Head banner flew over the city, and Wolf Soldiers in their grey tunics walked its walls, manned it towers, secured its safety against any invader.

The *House of Stowe* as the guide ship turned to bring its mighty hull across the prevailing current running directly into the harbor from the Safe River. The Wolf Soldier sailors tacked the ship mightily to the West, the gunwales threatening the Lake's black water, both horses snorting and stomping in fear as their world shifted.

Lee ran to Singer and Hectaro to Bastard. The fox ran back and forth across the rear of the ship, stepping in their horses' fresh manure, whimpering at the waves. As Lee stroked her horses neck, she stroked the foxes mind, letting it know safety was aboard the ship, not leaping from it.

The Confluni ship caught the current and dashed into the open maw of the city's harbor. Stone and timber bastions sized for Sea Wolves loomed up to either side of them. Harbor hands hung like monkeys from shipping lines, waiting to make the small ship fast, to bring it in to the safety of the space under the docks where the obsidian shelf of Wisex had been carved into a natural break water.

A breeze rose up behind them, and a line to the new sail leapt from the hands of one of the Wolf Soldiers responsible for it. The ship lurched first to port, then to starboard as the quartermaster overcompensated with the tiller. Lee heard the hull grind on the rock below the water and, to her horror, saw the boards in the hull move.

"Breach!" she screamed, the instinct being as natural to her as calling out 'Horse Free' when a mount escaped its stall in the stables. She pointed with a shaky finger at the boards in the hull that were already passing water.

"War's beard!" one of the Wolf Soldiers swore, the one who'd dropped the line. As another gathered it, the one at fault ran for the breach with a board and a hammer, to patch the flow for long enough to allow them to moor.

He put the board in place, he positioned a nail, and he struck it with his hammer. The board, nail, hammer and all went through the hull and a geyser of cold water sprayed them all.

Bastard called out his challenge and reared. The fox gathered itself and leapt from the ship toward the lower slip where the harbor hands had been guiding them. Lee called out after it with her mind, then saw its front claws take the wooden boards, its rears scrabbling up behind. A surprise to both her and the fox, one of the deck hands took it by the scruff of the neck and pulled him up the rest of the way.

The horses were not so lucky. Bastard returned to all-fours and immediately mule-kicked the side of the boat, shattering more wood. Singer called her challenge, the water up to her fetlocks, and tried to rear.

Wolf Soldiers were leaping from the boat to the dock. One came for Lee. "There's no saving them now, miss," he said. "Come with me and I'll get ye to the boards."

"No!" she told him, her hands on Singer's reins. She exchanged a look with Hectaro. Both horses were in trouble and Bastard was gathering for another kick.

The Wolf Soldier took her around the waist. He'd save her no matter what she said, she knew. A Wolf Soldier pledges his or her life to Lupus, her father, and then to her family.

"No!" she half-hissed and half-roared. This was the last Wolf Soldier on board, the rest having saved themselves, leaving Hectaro to make his own decisions.

One was enough to save a Princess.

"No!"

She focused her will. She exercised her power. No spell, no incantation – just will to save herself, Hectaro, this Wolf Soldier and the horses.

With a snap and a flash they were standing on wooden boards of dock, her fox racing for her, the Confluni ship sinking, its hull being dashed again and again against the rock walls by the prevailing current.

The same Wolf Soldier stood between her and the fox, pulling his sword. Her tiny hand clamped down on his shoulder.

"That fox is mine," she informed him. "On your *life*, no harm comes to it."

The Wolf Soldier subsided, his training taking over in the emergency. "On my life, my Lady," he informed her.

Singer subsided, now on more familiar dry land, and that was a good thing, because Lee needed to take a fist full of her mane just to keep her feet.

***

Lee and Hectaro stayed in the family tower in the palace at Wisex. Hectaro slept in the bed earmarked to be her brother's normally. She slept in the one reserved for herself, for the first time ever. The room sported a separate bath much like her chambers in Galnesh Eldador, and she made good use of it.

An Uman lady in waiting was recruited for her, and the girl styled her wild hair, and put poultices on the scars on her body which would benefit from them, and fit her for a palace dress and proper shoes.

By the morning of the 12th day of Water, she was once again a proper Princess sitting in a court of two, her audience the Wolf Soldier general Tagamack, a Volkhydran with uncharacteristic short hair and clean-shaven face, clearly more of a Hydran lineage.

He dressed in red hose and a yellow tunic, his grey tabard looking out of place on him, steel sleeves and greaves his sign of office.

Her called her, "My Lady," and put the entire city at her disposal. Would she like another mount, more food or wine, more servants? Would she like to send a message to her mother and father?

"We can't use Central Communications," he said. "It stopped working the day you – um, on the day you escaped the King of Trenbon. We're back to pigeons and fast riders, like the savages."

He added that with a smile, then realized 'the savages' were usually Andarons, and those were her people, as well.

"What's your compliment of Sea Wolves?" she asked him. They were seated in a tower in the palace, at the center of the city, where she could see out through great, open windows into the city with its black stone and black buildings.

"Just the two," the general informed her, "And we're desperate for them. We rarely send them up the Safe River, never down the Mid."

"My father sends a steady stream of supplies here," Lee argued. They sat at a round table, fruit, nuts and wine laid out for their pleasure. Hectaro had taken all three, and Lee surprised herself by joining him.

She'd had wine but not enjoyed it. Now it seemed like it replenished her energies.

General Tagamack nodded. "We have several barges, drawn by aurochs, travelling up and down the Safe River," he said. "Andarons know not to bother them. From the mouth of the Safe, you can catch a launch out of Chatoos or, if you're lucky, there's a Sea Wolf or two.

"But the last launch is in less than two hours," he said. "If you want to leave on it, we can make you ready, but we cannot delay."

"What?" Hectaro said, standing. "You're telling the *Imperial Princess* that you can't accommodate her?"

The general's face scrunched up in a squint, his brown eyes dashing between them. "My apologies," he said, "but we're at war, and war plans are unforgiving. If the barge doesn't leave on time, it can't leave at all. The river will be impassable."

Lee regarded Hectaro. Her father had designs on Andoron, but things must have gone exceptionally well in Volkhydro if he was engaging them now. She nodded.

"Have us ready," she informed the general. "By all means."

Chapter Thirty-One

Just a Little Bit of War

Lee and Hectaro both agreed to leave Singer and Bastard in the stables in Wisex. She could call for them later as she had before, she knew. As well, there were portals between this city and Galnesh Eldador if she chose to use them to retrieve both mounts.

She could have used them now, but she knew her father wasn't in the capitol, and she didn't want to resume those duties yet if she didn't have to. As a Mordetur, her first duty was to let her parents know she was still alive, and she could best accomplish her goal at the mouth of the Safe River if her father meant to take Chatoos.

The barge was cramped and smelled of old wood and urine. It was barely loaded when travelling up the Mid River, making it easier on the aurochs to pull it, and so it hadn't been packed with much more than travel fare as an emergency in case the pulling team lost theirs.

It took a week for them to travel up the river, the aurochs being much more energetic than oxen. It rained twice but it didn't seem to disturb any of them.

Lee had dressed once again in her travel clothes, her leather riding pants and boots, a burgundy blouse and a blue travel cloak. They'd retailored the Emperor's clothes to fit Hectaro and he looked quite dashing in the brown leather pants and white homespun shirt the Emperor favored. His boots even had a chain across the instep, although he quickly removed it.

They arrived at the city of Chatoos to find it under siege by thousands of Eldadorian troops, those ringed by fewer thousands of Andaron riders.

"There must be twenty tribes here," Lee guessed, looking at them from the Andoron side of the Safe River.

"And no less than 25,000 Eldadorians," Hectaro added. He pointed at the walls of Chatoos. "But look – the city has moved all of its defenses to the east. If they think they'll just march in there and take it, they've got another thing coming."

Lee's father was notorious for winning against logical odds, but not for attacking foolishly. Chatoos' strength lay in its ability to see any enemy coming. Its back to the Safe River, it would take more troops than this to overwhelm her defenses, even without the Andarons who would be buzzing the attackers.

"No," she said, shaking her head. "No, this isn't right. There is more to this than we can see."

"Well, I know what I can see," Hectaro said, "and we aren't marching into that camp. If the Andarons would pass us, and not take us as hostages, then the Eldadorians would kill us before we could tell them who we are."

Lee shook her head. She knew she was enough her mother's daughter to get past the Andarons into the Eldadorian camp – and then to her father.

But it wasn't her father's banner flying over the blue-and-white striped pavilion at the center of the Eldadorian camp. Her father's banner was the same wolf's head they all used, but only his had red eyes.

No, if Lee wasn't mistaken, then her younger brother's banner flew down there.

It brought to mind the message she'd received from Clear Genna.

"We're supposed to leave," one of the Wolf Soldiers who guided the river launch said.

She turned to him. "What?"

He pointed to the mouth of the river. "If there's not a Sea Wolf there, and there's not," he said, "then we're to leave. 'Tis the 19th of Water, and the attack comes on the 21st. No one can be on the Safe on the 21st."

"Why is that?" Hectaro asked.

Lee held up her hand. He wouldn't know. And if he did, he wouldn't say. He wouldn't endanger their lives with such knowledge.

"Go," she told them.

The two Wolf Soldiers regarded each other.

She eyeballed them quietly. They meant to return with her. Lee Mordetur had other things to do.

"Perhaps…" Hectaro began.

She shook her head.

All three males sighed.

"Give us what provisions you don't need for the trip back," she said. "We just strolled through the plains and the mountains of Conflu – we'll be fine in Andoron."

***

She ended up using the barge to cross the Safe River. With the two armies here, the Confluni were likely thick in the woods on this side, but Lee felt she could handle their groups of ten more easily than Andaron thousands.

They hadn't gone a daheer before she realized the mistake she had made.

They'd entered a little glen with a rock outcropping and a natural spring in it, and she was about to tell Hectaro to refill their water skins, when she saw a shadow cross the water. The shadow had a head and arms.

She told her fox to hide in the woods, and she looked up into the trees.

Confluni didn't move like this, but she knew who did.

"You can come down," she said, in Aschire.

Hectaro first gripped the pommel of his sword, then pulled his hand away from it. He hadn't even suspected who was there; he just recognized the language.

A dozen Aschire, both males and females, dropped down out of the trees. It made sense her father would have watchers in these woods, and he knew the best.

"You recognized me," she said to the male with a long, white strand of birch bark woven into his purple hair. He was the leader of the tribe.

"We did," he said, the surprised look on his face not betraying his anger, except to Lee, who knew how to read an Aschire. "Or you'd be dead."

She nodded. She didn't extend her hand to greet them – the Aschire didn't like to be touched.

"I have to find my father and mother," Lee informed them. If anyone could get them into Vulpe's camp, it would be the Aschire.

The Aschire shook his head. "No," he said. "You don't."

Lee cocked an eyebrow. "Don't I?" she asked him.

The Aschire were very loyal to her father, but they had their own ways. Sometimes when they spoke, always blunt and to the point, it was easy to misinterpret them.

"No," he said, "there is another you will speak to. Then you'll be on a ship to Galnesh Eldador."

Lee looked surprised. She wasn't going to interfere with her father's closest allies two days before what was going to be a very difficult battle, either.

"I'll follow you," she said, and stepped back.

He nodded. "See that you do."

***

There were a lot of people whom Lee might have expected to meet in the woods in Conflu.

Nina of the Aschire wasn't one of them. She still dressed in her leather pants and harness, she still wore the same daggers on her arms and thighs, but one look at Nina told Lee she was totally different from the girl who'd watched over her for her entire life.

They didn't embrace, as they might have in the privacy of the Imperial Palace. Aschire don't like to be touched, and Nina was with her people now.

But her eyes twinkled with love for her charge, and Lee knew Nina well enough to know she was thanking her Aschire forest for Lee still being alive.

"You are well to meet," Nina said. "I am glad the news of your death was false."

Lee wanted to burst into tears and run into Nina's arms, but she held herself rigid and formal, a Princess addressing a servant of the realm. "You trained me how to survive."

As big a complement as she could pay Nina, and said before a few dozen of her kinsmen, who would repeat it.

Nina nodded. "You can't go to Chatoos," she said. "You can't visit your brother, either. We have no way to get you in there."

Lee would never call Nina a liar, but her words just didn't ring true. "The Imperial house –" she began.

"I am no longer a member," she said, "of the Imperial house."

Lee gasped despite herself. She never thought she see a day of her life when Nina wouldn't be among the Mordetur's. She and her mother were almost sisters to her.

"I will see your father, and I will let him know you are well," she said.

Lee opened her mouth, but Nina continued. "You need to go to Galnesh Eldador, and there is a Sea Wolf to take you. In my rooms, you'll find a sword and shield I think you need to have."

"What?" Lee was a sorceress. What use did she have for a sword and shield?

"I found them in Volkhydro," she said, "and I carried them to your father. When I saw him, there was a harpoon your mother had, and then another of his allies, Arath, had a sword with a bone handle.

"The sword and shield galled me," she said. "Your mother said the same of the harpoon and Arath his sword. What's more, I met a man…"

Nina stumbled over her words, her eyes wandered for a moment. She'd met a male, Lee thought, and he had made quite an impression.

"He wields a black sword, and it is unlike any I've seen," Nina continued. "Now I think you need to see the sword and shield I found, that I had sent to Galnesh Eldador.

"There is something coming, Lee," Nina concluded. "Something bigger than what we're seeing. We know the gods are involved in this, and I think you need to be home in Galnesh Eldador."

Lee had to agree. She'd heard Glynn Escaroth sing a song of weapons, and now weapons were showing up.

That, and D'leer's words, were forming a path in her mind.

Lee nodded. Without a second look at Hectaro, she said, "Take me to the ship."